JAMES DAMM

The Superhero's Murder

First edition

This book was professionally typeset on Reedsy.
Find out more at reedsy.com

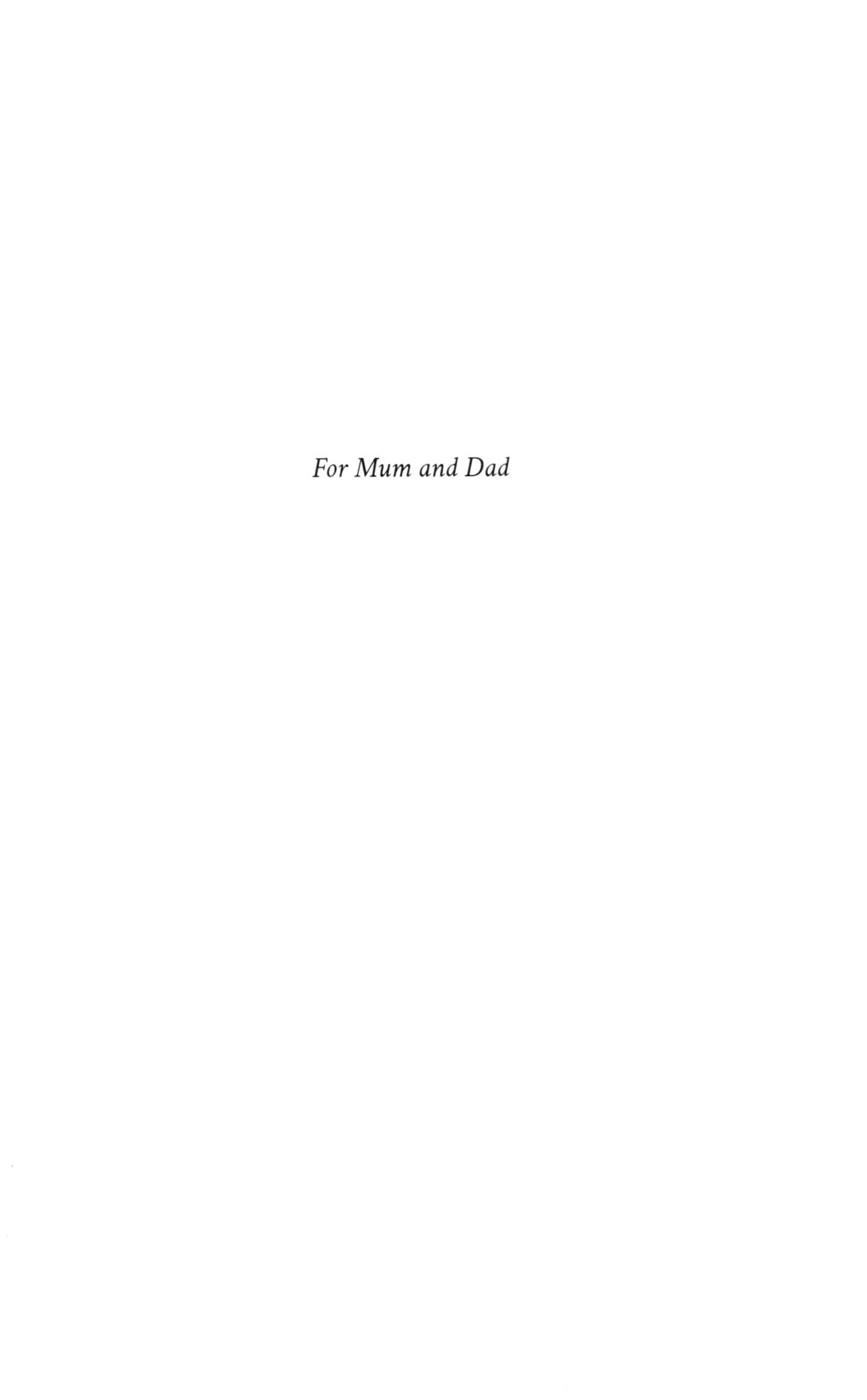

For Mum and Dad

Contents

Prologue

In Cherwell School's Year Eleven English class, twenty-nine sets of eyes scanned the clock on the far wall. Mr. Baker, the youngest and therefore most enthusiastic English teacher in the department, did his best to maintain the energy levels in the room. Before his class, he danced as if performing on a stage. Prancing and jumping before his audience of jaded fifteen-year-olds, Emma Hale admired his commitment to a lost cause.

With a textbook re-purposed as a fan, Emma dragged the pages back and forth, attempting to create any kind of airflow. The top floor classroom they occupied had a miserable reputation: pupils knew D floor as the sauna, while the less polite referred to it as hell on earth. For generations, students trudged up the single staircase to a classroom, never able to maintain a temperature to please anyone. In winter, students trembled in the icy air, while in summer they sweltered.

The classroom was four floors up and the windows only slid open so far, planned in such a way that a rogue, rebellious student would struggle to squeeze out. A single fan battled against the humidity, but only wafted scorching air from one place to another. With skin soaked with sweat underneath shirts, ties, and blazers, the students had learnt little in the previous forty minutes.

"Sir, can we go outside?" Grant Rogers pleaded from the side. "I think I'm going to die."

Mr. Baker laughed as his hands fell to his hips. With the mess of curls on his head damp, sweat patches visible all over his shirt, and panting slightly, he could sympathise with the students. All day the school time-tabled him for lessons in the sauna. The lack of rotation was a present for being the newest teacher in the building. Nothing would delight him more than taking the class outside to bathe in the sun, but experience taught Emma that such thoughts would never become a reality. The new teachers always stuck to the lesson plan; they were too green and keen to impress.

"At the start of the lesson I said anybody who needs a trip downstairs to fill their water bottle is more than welcome," Mr. Baker stated. "I know it's hot in here, but for you it's only for one lesson. Imagine being me in here all day."

Muttering between students acknowledged that the rawest deal of them all belonged to Mr. Baker. But as a teacher, he didn't count. The school paid him to be there.

Grant groaned and banged his head against the desk, his tie loose around his neck and with a blank sheet of paper and no pen before him. The lesson had taken its toll on the student. Mr. Baker admired that Grant turned up at all. "Can I please go fill my water then, sir?"

"Yes, you can Grant," Mr. Baker assured. "But I know it's a five-minute round trip to the bottom floor cooler. Don't be any longer."

Grant slid up from his seat and slunk out of the room. An invisible, unspoken knowledge among the class existed that the trip would be a ten-minute one. Long enough to take the piss and impress his fellow students, not long enough to get him into actual trouble. Emma considered that Grant would learn as much outside the classroom, anyway. A fan of football, wrestling and video games, his school-work got in the way of his real passions.

The lesson continued, and Mr. Baker looked for a volunteer to read the next section of the book. The book in question, *The Lord of the Flies*, was hated by the class. They all found Piggy to be an annoying character, and came up with many jokes about his death. During a previous lesson, Mr. Baker had held his head in his hands, mock-crying at the consensus of the class that Piggy deserved everything he got.

A classroom full of eyes avoiding making eye contact with the teacher, Henry Bell ended up being the first to buckle. After he held up a nervous arm to volunteer, so began the painstaking narration from one of the least adept readers in the class. Five minutes of mispronounced and stuttered sentences almost made Emma wish she had volunteered. Almost.

Out of nowhere the fire alarm sounded, and a universal cheer erupted up from the class. Mr. Baker slammed his book down on the desk, his expression one of relief and appreciation for whoever had put them out of their misery. Henry Bell beamed and discarded his own book to the floor. The situation would mean ten minutes on the tennis court, by which point the lesson, or torture, would be all but over.

"Everybody leave your stuff and head single-file out of the classroom," Mr. Baker called over the excited chatter of his pupils.

Near the back, Emma gestured relief to a nearby friend and meandered towards the exit. One hand on the wood,

Mr. Baker propped the door open as one by one the students filtered into the corridor.

"Smoke," a voice recognisable as Angela's screamed, causing the queue to freeze in its tracks.

Reputation established Angela as responsible and serious, not a pupil to fool around. Mr. Baker darted out the room. In seconds pupils with frightened faces, and in a state of panic, headed back inside.

"Back inside the classroom," Mr. Baker barked with an urgency in his voice that sent the last of the pupils scampering.

He slammed the door and grabbed his jacket from his chair. Frantic hands placed the jacket underneath the gap in the frame. Light smoke, a kind more similar with burning toast, filtered in visibly through the gaps in the frame. Mr. Baker emptied the contents of his water bottle onto the jacket.

"We need to stay low," Mr. Baker urged as his tone softened and he led the way into a crouch. "With me, stay low to the ground."

A classroom of pupils followed the teacher's lead to the letter. Once happy every pupil was crouched low enough, Mr. Baker moved toward the window. He snatched a discarded hoody from the floor and waved it out the window to draw attention.

The rest of the eyes in the room fell on the closed door. A single jacket lay at its base. Grey smoke still entered through the sides of the old wooden frame.

"I could see fire on the staircase," Angela wept in earshot, her eyes red. "The flames were already so big."

The alarm sounded and in sixty seconds Archie Boyd and the rest of the crew at Cherwell Fire Station scrambled into engines. Down the poles, firefighting tunics, boots and helmets thrown on, they packed the cab without a pause for breath. Archie's freshly brewed tea would remain untouched.

Lights and sirens blaring, the first engine, followed by the second, swerved and manoeuvred through the late morning traffic. Multiple calls to the control centre pointed to a major incident at the local high school with no drill planned. A fire on the upper floors and children trapped. The cascaded information horrified the cab to silence.

The call had only reached the station five minutes earlier, but the sky above already showed signs of escalation. The driver's face was a picture of determination in control of the wheel as he navigated the traffic, weaving past any blockage. Nervous with anticipation, Archie rubbed his hands in an unconscious twitch. As they approached, they took in the sight of the blaze. How had it grown so fast?

"The children in there need us," Eric Chapman, the crew manager called out to the silent cab. "The threat of loss of life is high and nobody else is coming but us."

Children. The word pumped fear and adrenaline in equal measure through Archie's veins. As the engine pulled into the tennis court, the weight of the situation fell upon him.

Teachers shepherded pupils back with one eye on the building, black smoke billowing and flames licking out from the third-floor windows. On the floor above, an arm, hoodie in hand, waved from a window. The colourful green and blue panels that wrapped the building burned, the cladding exacerbating the blaze. Less than seven minutes from the initial calls, the fire had already half-circled the building.

Screeching, screaming and crying echoed across the tennis court. The crew manager passed instructions to get the pupils away from the scene and down the hill. They had a job to do and an audience would neither help the rescue nor themselves. This was a once-in-a-lifetime incident. Every firefighter trained for one, but no training could prepare them for the reality. In his stomach, all Archie knew was that the job of his career would be today.

Eric Chapman established command of the situation. With a fast-moving fire already out of control, the conditions would push his team and their equipment to the limit. The cladding on the exterior of the building pushed the flames higher, the fire leaping and dancing up the exterior walls. There could be no immediate rescue through external routes. The crew manager instructed Archie and two others to fit breathing apparatus. One staircase to the top floor had to be the principal route of rescue.

Cylinders of air strapped to his back like a rucksack, Archie pulled the mask to fit over his face and secured the straps around his head. A gauge on his shoulder strap would inform Archie of how much air, around thirty minutes' worth, remained in the tank. Registers collected by the teaching staff highlighted twenty-eight unaccounted for pupils, all trapped on the top floor.

While Archie and two others put on their equipment, Eric Chapman signalled for others to bring out the ladders. A standard engine contained four, the longest at thirteen and a half meters, which would be able to reach the top-floor window and create another escape route. They would tackle the fire now raging on the outside before carrying down those trapped.

The final firefighters scattered for the hose jet, which required two to operate and would hopefully tackle the blaze enough to ease the conditions inside.

The task understood, and breathing apparatus attached, Archie and the crew jogged inside. "This isn't London," Eric reminded Archie and the crew. "We have two engines in operation. They will dispatch more, but this is the best we have for now."

Twenty-eight pupils and their teacher were trapped inside. As Archie and his fellow firefighters thundered towards the entrance, a single elemental thought settled in his head and that of every firefighter. Every single firefighter within that building would lose their own life to save those trapped. Every single one.

On the ground floor, smoke filled the corridor. With little time to adjust, Archie took in a quick view of lockers, deserted benches and displays of the pupils' work lining the walls. The staircase before them climbed all the way to the top floor. And the trapped children.

With each step the smoke became darker, the heat intensifying. After the first floor, visibility became poor, and Archie became reliant on touch to guide his way. With a hand placed on the left-hand wall, the firefighters moved in single file and used the brickwork to navigate. By the time they approached the second floor, screaming filled the darkness. Archie's heart pounded in his chest as he moved blind through the devastation.

Radio reports coming through highlighted the third floor as ground zero, the source of the fire a bin on the staircase. A pupil in a tearful state admitted to the act of arson; his innocent enough aim was to set off a fire alarm and get his class out of their English lesson on the top floor. When he returned from refilling his water bottle, the fire raged out of control. The pupil smashed the alarm. Stupidity knew no boundaries.

Via the radio, the crew manager instructed the breathing apparatus team to continue upwards. Outside, the building was engulfed in flames. Inside the staircase remained the only immediate route of escape.

Reaching the third floor, Archie felt the general heat hitting in those areas. Not like a burn, but a wave of heat that made his face tingle. The breathing apparatus mask limited his vision, the black roaring smoke not helping either, but the heat of the fire was unmistakable as his body sweltered.

Pushing on to the top floor, they smashed the sole door open and entered a classroom black from the smoke.

"Stay low, STAY LOW!" Archie yelled as he scooped up one pupil from the floor and then another. As teenagers, they were light enough to carry, but were weighed down heavier in the conditions. "Stay where you are, help is on its way."

Making a swift exit from the room, Archie headed back down the staircase. At this point other firefighters had hauled a hose up the stairs and attacked the source of the original fire. The small relief the water generated meant before Archie knew it, he was back onto the ground floor. He handed the two soot-covered bodies to paramedics now on scene. In the chaos, Archie could not determine whether the girls had been alive or dead.

A scan of his shoulder gauge showed more than half a tank left, and once more Archie hauled himself up the darkened staircase. Radio chatter warned that the outside of the building had become an impenetrable wall of fire, the cladding now a cloak of heat.

Archie hauled a larger male, he presumed the teacher, out of the room and toward the stairs. He regretted that he could only take one person on his second trip. The physical effect of the heat had taken its toll and his body was fatigued underneath the suit.

Down and down the stairs Archie dashed, and as he did so his suit whistled, indicating his oxygen was running out. It would be the last trip until he could get hold of a new kit.

Upon reaching the bottom of the stairs, paramedics dived forward to grab the limp body. Important to release the heat after an incident like this, Archie opened his tunics and took off the flash hood. Police took the initial trio of firefighters out of the building under the police shields. Debris from the exterior crashed down, and they made their way to the safe area.

Archie broke down his breathing apparatus set and serviced it in the safe area. After use, he needed to change the oxygen cylinders and make sure that the fire hadn't damaged the sets. Unsure whether it was the adrenalin coursing through his system, or the physical exertion of going up and down the stairs, Archie felt exhausted. More crews and engines had arrived and as he re-hydrated, they dashed past and up the stairs. Soot-covered bodies of school children were either carried or dragged out. He could not gauge how many they had got to. Preparing himself for going back into the building, a glance up at the ball of flame and black smoke turned his stomach.

The classroom got darker and darker. In minutes the fire forced Mr. Baker to abandon signalling from the window as flames moved up on the outside. He retreated down to the floor as grave concern filled his face. With a glance upwards, Emma could not make out the ceiling as the smoke in the room had become so dense and black. That smoke entered from the outside, not inside, and the decision to stay put and await the firefighters constantly stirred in her brain.

Emma herself tried to yell out, but smoke blew into her face and she couldn't help but inhale it. The black smoke burnt her eyes and throat, the saving grace being that it wasn't so hot that it hurt her skin. The fire itself licked the external windows, the fire inside yet to be visible.

As the minutes ticked by, firefighters burst into the room, visible only from the knee down. Towards the back of the classroom Emma witnessed as they scooped students up and hauled them out of the room. Almost as soon as they appeared, they disappeared again and the heat in the classroom kept rising. Eyes trained on the door, Emma felt powerless and kept herself on the ground.

Stay put had been the explicit instruction, but her eyes burnt and, as the smoke filled her lungs, panic took its toll. On the second trip they came for Mr. Baker, bodies emptying from the room as the solitude twisted her thoughts. They would not reach her in time. Emma's lungs felt suffused with smoke, her limbs limp with fatigue. She had to get out.

Frantic, she spotted the gap in the window from earlier and crawled towards it, not being able to contemplate another minute in the furnace that tortured Emma's body and scratched her lungs. The fall would kill her, but the terror of the burning to death outweighed everything. Head out first, then shoulders, Emma's mind could not comprehend the pain as the fire bit and tore at her skin. She had to get out. She had to get free. Adrenaline in charge, she pushed out as hard as she could.

"No, no, no, no, NO!" Archie yelled as he watched the body

drop out of the window. A jumper. The body tumbled down through the air and in horror the firefighter expected to hear the thump as he clenched his eyes shut. Yet when he pried them open, nobody lay visible on the ground. No thud echoed in his ears.

Archie's eyes darted between the window where he had just witnessed the figure jump and the ground where he expected to see an impact. Was he going mad? A quick glance to his left and right and the expressions on his colleagues' faces showed they had seen the same thing. Yet their eyes focused on something.

When Archie's attention refocused on the scene, a single figure, a man, stood in the air opposite the window. Physically exhausted and dehydrated, Archie could not process fast enough the scene before him. Like a puppet-master pulling strings, the fire tamed and danced to the moving hands of the man. A sudden jerk and the flames before him extinguished entirely. The fire engulfed the building one second, and then only smoke remained a moment after.

Another second passed and Archie watched the man rip a window from its frame and toss it like a simple tennis ball. The figure disappeared into the gap and emerged with two bodies under either arm, floating down to the waiting paramedics. Without pause for breath, he repeated his task again and again, the assembled crowd watching in awe.

It would have only been a minute until the classroom stood empty. Firefighters readjusted themselves and continued to dash back to their previous jobs – hoses in hands and streams of water firing, they brought the remnants of the fire under control. Archie remained rooted to the spot.

The figure approached a paramedic nearby and jumped into the back of the ambulance before its doors swung shut. There was no question about his right to be there. Brown hair, soot-covered skin, tears in his clothes, yet nothing that resembled a burn. A jacket, a t-shirt and no firefighting tunic. The person who combated the fire wore no protection at all. He was just a man; a person Archie would not bother to look twice at in the street.

"Who the fuck was that?" Archie quizzed his colleagues.

"The guy about to get all the credit," Robert Jackson replied as he slapped a hand on Archie's shoulder. "Let's go see what the boss needs."

The paramedics ripped what remained of any school uniform from Emma's body and forced her to lay flat on her back. The setting resembled an ambulance, although Emma could only be half-aware of all the surrounding activity. An oxygen mask over her face, a line prodded into her left arm with what she presumed was a drip. Her vision could not settle in the chaos.

Eyes panicked, Emma wanted them to cry but found not an ounce of fluid in her body available to do so. She wanted to call for her mum, but her throat felt arid and her lips swollen.

What happened? Terror of the fire, terror of falling, and then there she lay, alive but in agony. There were two paramedics rushing around, yelling instructions at each other she could not distinguish. Yet at the back of the confined space, Emma could see a man who looked like he had been in the fire himself. Dishevelled, clothes torn and soot blackening his skin, the man looked on with concern and hesitation.

Upon making eye contact with him, the man paused and then reached forward, lightly grasping Emma's arm. "I should have been quicker."

Who was the man? Emma's memories skipped back to the

classroom, Henry Bell, Angela and Mr. Baker. She had no idea who had lived and who had died. The man was no teacher, no fireman. Why was he there and how had he been in the fire?

"You're doing great," he assured her. "My name's John. I'm the person who caught you and I will stay with you until I know you're safe, if that's okay?"

Emma agreed as much with her eyes. Out the window she had fallen, flames licking at her skin and hair. Then the falling had stopped.

Chapter One

Where were you on the day of the superhero's murder?

Every person alive had their own answer. In every lifetime, the odd event occurs that is so monumental that people could remember where they were, when they heard the news. A rare moment so striking that it forces a person to take stock and mark the memory.

In her lifetime Juliet had encountered several days which historians claimed changed the world. Princess Diana's death happened when she was too young to appreciate the true significance of it, yet the memory remained all the same. 9/11? A teenager by that point, Juliet could remember watching the footage of the hijacked planes hitting the World Trade Center, and the fear that had filled the pit of her stomach on doing so. Five years later, there was the footage of the Cherwell fire rescue, and the revelation that a superhero lived among them. Several days frozen in time.

Yet none felt like the day they discovered John Fitzgerald's body. That same superhero from the fire found brutally stabbed to death. Yet John Fitzgerald's murder felt bigger than one country or society. Those other memorable days belonged to the West – the US and Europe. What impact did 9/11 have on the average citizen in Kenya? Did a Sri Lankan, living amidst their civil war, care for a wall's collapse in Germany? John Fitzgerald lived as a global figure, his death as universally recognised as the person who'd lived it. *Where were you on the day of the superhero's murder?*

At the start of the day, Juliet ran. Half an hour in, she would go at least another hour. Catching a glance at the mirror that lined the wall, Juliet noticed her beet-red cheeks and a toned frame pounding the treadmill. Once those cheeks acted as a point of shame. Before her teenage years, where everything changed, Juliet flushed red at the slightest cue. A hint of embarrassment, anxiety, or being too hot. When she'd sense the colour of her face changing, Juliet used to bite down on the inside of her cheeks as hard as she could, determined to hide her tell. Sometimes Juliet bit so hard that the taste of blood would fill her mouth.

Now Juliet's red cheeks stood out as one of her favourite features. When she looked up, and witnessed her beetroot face, she felt a kick. *That's someone who's working her arse off.* Nobody could look at Juliet while she exercised and doubt her commitment to the cause. Not that there was ever anyone to challenge that commitment. Approaching six in the morning, the only other person in the gym confined himself to the weights area: headphones in, furrowed brow, grunting as he worked out. He was the type whose biggest concern they allowed themselves in the gym was what the next exercise was – the perfect partner.

Fitness had not always been a passion of Juliet's; it was only in the last few years that she had even stepped inside a gym for the first time. From there, the commitment grew and exploded. Five times a week she'd be dead-lifting, clean and press-ing, swimming, cycling, or using whatever piece of equipment she wanted to master. Juliet dedicated days to competitions, diet and exercise, or planning out a route to personal best-times. Last year she'd run the London Marathon in less than four hours, and soon Juliet aimed to make that time look like child's play. A relentless regime had taken over her life as Juliet yanked her body to its physical limits.

As Juliet's feet pounded the treadmill, she heard a snippet of what was to come. A man she knew all too well had entered the gym and flashed a badge at the receptionist. No small talk, no delay. The figure demanded the receptionist open the barrier and hurried in Juliet's direction.

Tom Harper's dominating frame was his most distinguishing feature. At six foot four, the man used to box in his youth, long ago, but the build and structure of his body had never abated. A man that could handle himself, both mentally and physically. This was apt, seeing as his chief role was that of Juliet's handler. When you're tall, you either cower away from your height or embrace it and all the intimidation that comes with it. As the door swung open and Tom came through, his familiar stride showed utter confidence, yet his face displayed a grave expression of somebody rattled. Juliet slowed the treadmill down to a walking pace the moment the expression registered.

"Another marathon?" Tom questioned as he approached.

"It's an Iron Man next," Juliet replied.

"What's one of those when it's at home?"

"A 2.4-mile swim, a 112-mile bicycle ride and a marathon run," Juliet answered.

The revolted expression on Tom's face articulated his

thoughts perfectly.

"It clears my head," she finished.

"Have you tried drinking instead?"

Juliet laughed as she got off the treadmill. She'd planned for a hybrid session of all three before work. Her plans had changed.

"Do I have time to shower?"

"You have five minutes, tops."

"Terrorist attack?"

"Worse."

John Fitzgerald. Juliet got the message as she stepped down off the treadmill and grabbed both her bottle and a towel. The pair stalked out of the gym at a pace.

"Where are we off to?"

"The crime scene."

Not wanting to keep him waiting, Juliet showered, changed into her white shirt, suit jacket and trousers, all within her allocated five minutes. Her employers had never interrupted a gym session of Juliet's before. With John Fitzgerald and a crime scene involved, the situation had already hit a severe level. At that point she wondered – who had he killed?

People other than John Fitzgerald possessed superpowers. The reason Tom interrupted Juliet's workout at six in the morning was because of hers. Juliet could read people's minds, the only known person on the planet who could do so. A member of the UK's Investigative Support Unit, Juliet assisted police in their enquiries, predominantly with interviews and contextual evidence-gathering.

As Juliet exited the changing room, she locked eyes and smiled at the bewildered receptionist she knew as Darren. His hair always unkempt and the rest of him in a constant state of disarray, he manned the desk most mornings. Yet a welcome hello and a warm smile greeted Juliet daily, despite his often-dishevelled aesthetic. To other people, Darren seemed just a normal bloke who potentially struggled to wake up in the morning. But from what Juliet had pieced together over the years, Darren's mum had dementia and he acted as her primary carer. Despite the comforting welcome behind the smile, she could see his fears for his mum's wellbeing or distressing fresh moments preying on his mind. Every morning before work he'd wake, bathe, feed and dress his elderly mother, before leaving her in the hands of a carer who could come later. The friendly receptionist had his own life, and own story masked behind a welcoming smile. There was no one *normal,* Juliet had learned. There were seven billion versions of normal on this planet. And she could read the minds of them all.

Being a person who could read minds, there was nothing lonelier in the world than being surrounded by a load of people on a different wavelength. Not only did Juliet have her own thoughts, the unfiltered access to everyone else's bombarded her. The mind, especially to those oblivious to who Juliet was, existed as an unruly entity. People presumed whatever went on inside was safe and theirs, whereas someone like Juliet could learn an entire person like Darren's back story without even exchanging a word with him. To other people, she walked around and carried such a power like nothing at all. In reality, she walked around with her head on fire and no one else able to see the flames. There was a reason she exercised alone so early in the morning.

Through the gym's barriers and out the main entrance, a black saloon car waited with two police cars, one at the front and one at the rear. With flashing lights, it would be a full police escort through London.

"Tom, what is this–" Juliet began before she had even hit the seat.

"Someone has murdered John Fitzgerald."

"Murdered?" The same sentence he'd just articulated verbally sat front and centre of his mind. She'd heard John's name and presumed he'd been the perpetrator.

Bulletproof. Indestructible. Superhuman strength. Those were the words she associated with John. Snippets of footage often circulated on television news or online with him in the heat of action, saving lives and performing acts of heroism so death-defying they looked straight out of a movie. Juliet's mind replayed the images over and over, and a murder contrasted with what she knew. No matter how long she imagined a murder scene, it seemed unbelievable with the victim involved.

"What the hell happened?"

The look Tom shot back in retort was clear. *That's what we're here to help find out.*

"Why the crime scene?" Juliet quizzed aloud. "Do we have somebody in custody?"

"Leave no stone unturned," Tom regurgitated. "That was the instruction the bosses gave me twenty minutes ago. Whenever we catch who did this, and we will, you'll be right there in the interview room making this case the most watertight we've ever seen. I want you to soak up everything, the crime scene, and every other part of this unreal day. Even a fraction of something you see today might trigger something later. We can't take a chance of anything being missed. Not with something like this."

As always, Juliet would be there to help gather intelligence rather than evidence. Crime scene officers would bag up evidence and collate all the forensics, and she would be there for the context – sharing nuggets of information that may prove invaluable in an interview later. The output from Juliet's mind reading couldn't be used in court. Past cases had shown it best to use her ability to help accelerate and flesh out the investigation rather than negotiate the legal complexity of mind reading.

Juliet pulled out her phone and clicked onto the BBC news app. The leading story was concerning education reforms. So the news hadn't broken yet. For what could only be a matter of hours, the world hadn't woken up to its grim new reality.

"They'll gag the press until they can make an official announcement," Tom said as he looked over. "Like the Queen's death, there will be an official announcement."

"Where are we heading to?" Juliet asked as she looked at empty streets pass by. Full blue lights, sirens blaring, the convoy cut through London at a rapid pace.

"They found the body in Tower Hamlets, near Devons Road Station."

Located east of the city, Hackney sat to the north of Tower Hamlets with the Thames to the borough's south. The borough hosted the world headquarters of many global financial businesses, employing some of the highest-paid workers in London, but also had the second-highest unemployment rate and the lowest life expectancy. The difference in lives a stone's throw away from each other was obvious and stark. As Juliet looked out the window once more, she could see the iconic glass skyscrapers looming in the skyline. Yet the buildings that quickly surrounded Juliet looked far different from the modern structures. Juliet had no idea how rough the area would feel at night; such information disguised by daylight.

The only thought Juliet noted as the convoy pulled to up to the location was that it looked relatively remote, an access road leading away from nearby flats and a pub. As Juliet stepped out of the car, she soaked in the scene. The pub and flats could be important for witnesses. The estimated time of death would be crucial to the likelihood of anybody seeing somebody enter or leave the access road. A sign on one of the warehouse lots advertised BESPOKE FURNITURE MAKERS, while others showed the road housed two garages and a concrete supplier – all operational businesses. There was no way a body would have stayed hidden for long.

"The sergeant declared life extinct twenty minutes ago," Tom said as he returned from speaking to the senior investigating officer in charge. "The photographer is in there at the moment before they let forensics in."

The photographer tried to capture the scene before anyone could disturb it, snapping the body from as many angles as possible. Juliet's mind flashed to pictures of JFK in the open-top car, Neil Armstrong posed before the US flag on the moon, the billowing black smoke of the World Trade Center on fire. Iconic scenes imprinted on the minds of those not even present. The photo of John Fitzgerald's body would surely be right alongside them.

A tent erected over the immediate scene, Juliet and Tom approached. To the side of the tent they pulled on the provided protective clothing: a set of overalls, latex gloves, paper shoes, and a face mask. Upon leaving the scene, one officer would collect all protective clothes worn throughout the investigation for analysis, to avoid the risk of losing valuable trace evidence. The situation still felt unreal, as if they would yank the doors of the tent open and reveal the entire thing was one big prank.

The moment those white tent doors revealed the scene, such thoughts evaporated. Slumped on his side facing Juliet, the body had a face recognisable to nearly every person on the planet. John Fitzgerald lay crumpled on the floor in a pool of blood, his black leather jacket, blue jeans and trainers all covered in it too.

This would be the spot where history changed. A tarmacked, unremarkable access road. As Juliet's eyes adjusted and focused on the still, lifeless body, so obviously John Fitzgerald, she could only wonder – what the hell had happened here?

Chapter Two

Later, when recalling the moment Juliet stood over John Fitzgerald's body, it was his eyes she remembered. There was no Hollywood moment where she moved forward to pull his eyelids down, the contamination of the body far too risky for that. Instead, John's eyes remained open, not haunted or wide, just empty as dead eyes were. Whatever made a person tick, whether a soul or otherwise, no longer existed in John. Juliet noted his eyes were teal-blue, but that didn't seem to matter anymore.

They were eyes that had seen things other human beings couldn't comprehend. When Haiti suffered one of the worst earthquakes of all time, with hundreds of thousands killed, John was there. The country's infrastructure devastated, John proved key to getting aid to remote areas and assisting with the relief effort in zones where standard equipment could not reach. That same year, an earthquake in Chile killed hundreds with John on the scene to rescue trapped casualties and make temporary infrastructure fixes to allow a wider relief effort. Those vacant eyes had seen more devastation than any other human being alive. As a nation, and a planet, they'd looked to John as a figure to clean up the messes and fix the problems.

Juliet knew all the above because she'd watched it on the news, tucked up, sheltered and safe in her own flat. The warmth, comfort and safety of a guardian had allowed the public to drift into a daydream where previous thoughts of terror resided.

But that dream was now over. The protector was dead.

Juliet's own gaze moved away from John's eyes to the rest of his body. The hair looked dishevelled while John's jawline sported whiskers that showed he hadn't bothered to shave for days. The white t-shirt he'd worn was in tatters, with punctures and holes joining the heavy scarlet stain. The number of holes suggested a frenzied stabbing. John's trainers were scruffy and old, his jeans just jeans, yet the jacket brought half a smile to Juliet's face. The superheroes in comics wore armour, masks and capes. Their superhero had worn a black leather jacket. *Always*.

Juliet continued to scrutinise the scene. The broken neck of a smashed wine bottle, caked in blood. The attacker dropped the weapon less than ten metres away, with a small yellow evidence marker now by its side. Shards of glass littered John's clothes and the ground around the body, with a trail of blood dotting the tarmac leading up to the where it lay.

To an investigator, the evidence should always guide the case, and there was no absence of material to work with around John Fitzgerald's body. First, the murder weapon of a broken wine bottle. Had the attacker clubbed John with the bottle? Did the bottle smash on impact or had the attacker dropped it? Had the attacker taken the opportunity and gone for the frenzied kill?

Who would have a wine bottle to hand? There was a pub round the corner. Officers would shortly round up and interview all those who'd been there last night in the hours before it closed. As Juliet scanned up and down the industrial road, there were no signs of other bottles or broken glass. Whoever had killed John had surely brought the bottle with them, at least a short distance.

Why had John been there? Such a frenzied attack. What was the chance that the superhero would be down this road and that a broken wine bottle would be the most effective weapon against him? Juliet supposed John Fitzgerald surprised the attacker down this road, sparking the confrontation and eventual murder.

But that failed to answer the most important question in Juliet's head: Had John Fitzgerald, of all people, really died just like that?

"I've watched footage of John deflecting bullets and moving through fire without a burn," Juliet stated as she and Tom removed their protective clothing. "How does he die from stab wounds from a broken bottle? Who even thinks to try it?"

Tom didn't answer as he removed the clothing. His thoughts were equally troubled, flicking between all these facts that already didn't add up.

"I don't know. But I think we'll catch whoever did it soon."

"How so?" Juliet asked.

"If you want to understand an artist, look at his work," Tom said as he motioned at the area with his arm. "This wasn't an assassination. The scene of the crime is littered with evidence from the body, the blood, to the murder weapon. Regardless of the time of death, the perpetrator won't have gotten far. It's a disorganised kill, feels in the moment, and there'll be CCTV all around with so many businesses nearby."

"Unless it's set up to look that way?"

"A possibility, but it disagrees with the rest of the scene," Tom acknowledged. "Did you see the lack of defensive wounds on his hands?"

Juliet had. "Maybe that means he knew his attacker, that or it was a blitz attack that took him by surprise."

Before either could continue their train of thoughts, the senior investigating officer approached. Tall, black, athletic, something about the way the man carried himself suggested he was former military – his posture and frame fixed. The confidence in his steps jarred with the thoughts inside his head. The man was nervous, the murder of the superhero landing on his desk was nobody's plan. Often called a red ball, the case would take precedence over existing active cases. They could and often made or broke a detective's career.

"Ethan," he said outstretching a hand which Juliet shook. "Anything you have that will save my sorry self?"

"Nothing you won't have already," Juliet replied. "I'll be of more value if we can get witnesses or a suspect into custody. Rattle their cages a little and I can see what falls out."

"We've already got officers speaking to the landlord of the pub down the road and any others nearby. We will question any punters that ordered bottles of wine or seemed suspicious. Plus, we'll look at their CCTV," Ethan said before pushing his luck. "Anything from those people over there?"

A small crowd formed at the blue police tape, curious to see inside the white tents that hid the crime scene from view. Their chattering thoughts were entirely out of curiosity, with no specific mention of John Fitzgerald. On an average Tuesday morning, nobody thought the road outside their home would have such far-reaching consequences within the world at large.

"Worth a shot," Ethan smiled as he watched Juliet shake her head. "The DLR station is being closed; I want the body out of here before too long. As soon as this story breaks, and it will, members of the public will come in their droves."

"Whatever we can do to help," Tom smiled.

Being a member of the UK's Investigative Support Unit, Juliet would assist police and intelligence agents in their enquiries, although her presence wasn't always welcome. The police managed and owned the case, and whichever detective they put in charge became the king or queen of proceedings. Even with a person like John Fitzgerald flying in the sky, Juliet had encountered many who considered her powers voodoo, over-egged or just plain unwanted.

Still, with hundreds of requests a year, neither Tom nor Juliet cared if some detectives never picked up the phone through stubbornness. There were plenty out there who wanted help, more cases than Juliet could ever handle. This obstinacy was especially true of old-school detectives who had been around a while, many of whom wanted to be left to their own devices. Sometimes the decision to bring in Juliet would go over their heads, a higher-up worried their team had become too blinkered. In those cases, Tom and Juliet needed to tread carefully through an unwelcome terrain. Often there were still results, but it made it harder, battling against the investigator and the case itself.

Rarely, but still out there, were those concerned with the morality of Juliet's power. Many believed they should designate the skull as a domain of absolute privacy. No one should be able to probe an individual's mind against their will, and law enforcement should forgo the use of Juliet's power, even though using it may serve the public good.

Ethan seemed to belong to the more accepting group. With no ego, he recognised that a case of this magnitude needed solving well and solving fast. Traditionally, to get a successful prosecution and conviction in a murder case, you need conclusive forensic evidence, eyewitness accounts, a confession, or good, strong circumstantial evidence. Ethan's attitude was to tick every box as thoroughly as possible. The acceptance of what Juliet could offer was refreshing.

"Later, when we've tracked down all those patrons from the pub, I'd appreciate you giving them the once-over with my detectives. Any patrons who last night left with a wine bottle or acted suspiciously, we'll see if anything marries up with the CCTV. Meanwhile, I have officers at John's flat, going through his possessions to ascertain who was in his inner circle. In all the chaos that will come, we can't forget the basics. Most murders are committed by somebody we know, somebody we love," Ethan said. "It may be Fitzgerald, but we need to approach it the same way. If possible, I'd like you to speak to the neighbours, get a sense of how often John was there, any familiar faces or overheard arguments. A simple way to track how he got to this road is to discover who he was with this past week."

"We can do that," Tom nodded as he looked to Juliet.

"Anything you specifically want us to look out for?" Juliet asked.

Ethan paused a second, his eyes involuntarily glancing over at the white tent. "Soak it all up, see what the neighbours say and anything suspicious you can find. But also keep an eye out for what's not there, anything missing that you'd usually expect."

The story of the murder broke ten minutes into the car journey. Social media users from the area had posted images of the white tent, asking if anybody knew what had happened. Half an hour later, one user proved to be the ignition and stirred the crowd up into a frenzy. The cousin of an officer told them it was John Fitzgerald. The absence of any acknowledgement by the mainstream media or why there was such a large police presence fanned the flames. His name began trending. The newspapers and mainstream voices remained silent. Foreign press, not gagged in the same way as the UK press, posted stories acknowledging the rumours and the sketchy details. What really caused the situation to stir was the announcement that at nine the Prime Minister would make a statement.

"What do you think of Ethan?" Juliet questioned as they drove past busying streets. It was approaching seven in the morning and more people were emerging for their commutes to work.

"A rising star, they've given the red ball to someone they want to see handle it well," Tom replied. "He was the SIO in the Patrick Goddard murder case. No forensics, no obvious suspects. He conducted one hell of an interview that eventually led to a full confession."

"Good, then?"

"Someone who will get this case solved fast."

The drive to John's home only took ten minutes: a penthouse suite on the forty-eighth and forty-ninth floor. As the car approached the change in scenery became obvious. Gone were the tightly congested flats near the crime scene. These apartments were at the complete other end of the scale, a starkly contrasting world.

As the car pulled up to the entrance, police officers were already stationed at the door, checking the identification documents of those entering. With rumours already beginning to circulate, it wouldn't take long for reporters or snoopers to rock up to John's place of residence to get some extra gossip.

A man just over thirty greeted the pair. "Toby Jones," a voice stated with an outstretched hand. "I'm the hospitality manager for the Invictus Building." Wearing a three-piece suit, smart watch and with a subtle hint of an expensive aftershave, the way Toby presented himself gave the impression of utmost professionalism. When dealing with millionaires, bankers and the entitled, the idea the 'customer is always right' went a step further.

"Tom Harper, and this is Juliet Reynolds. We're hoping to speak briefly with a few of the staff and neighbours."

Toby offered a tight smile, a false shield to protect himself from the wrath of the rich and powerful who could get him fired with one phone call.

"I can make the introductions," Toby assured them as he led them inside past the police officers. "We have an in-house team available to residents around the clock. Anybody you wish to speak to is available."

High-beamed ceilings, a significant water feature and trees greeted Juliet and Tom in the Invictus lobby. As Toby led them inside, he gave them the rundown of all the things a resident could expect living in the building. Garden sanctuaries throughout, an environment designed to make the best use of space and light. A residents' private cinema, swimming pool, rooftop observatory and sky lounge with dining facilities. At the heart of Canary Wharf, the building had views over the dock and a resident could happily spend days without venturing outside of its doors.

"A private sky garden?" Tom questioned aloud, confused.

"It's a simple difference, but a game changer: Invictus's

apartments do not just have balconies but fully fledged private gardens. The spacious exteriors mean the benefit of an expansive outdoor area, rare in such a central setting, is granted to each apartment. Not only that, the floor-to-ceiling windows create an enhanced sense of space even when you are inside," Toby enthused. "With the doors open, the private garden becomes an extension of the residence. The boundary between home and garden, comfort and discovery, can be exactly what you want it to be."

"You're not selling me the place, kid," Tom replied laughing and Toby became visibly dampened. *Prick* was the word Juliet could read at the forefront of Toby's mind, but she kept that knowledge to herself. The company rhetoric rehearsed down to a sentence, there'd be no open and honest conversations with any of the staff. Luckily Juliet didn't need one. As they approached the lift to the apartment, Toby fished out a key. Juliet made a mental note that to get access to John's top-floor apartment, you needed one.

"How often would John ever get the lift?"

"Rarely," Toby admitted. "It being the penthouse suite, he usually just flew in from above. He still received post and occasionally had guests though, so came up and down those days."

"Did he have guests often?"

Toby racked his brains, looking for the answer Juliet wanted to hear, and came up empty. The thoughts that stirred in his brain were that, despite John living there for four years, he'd only seen the man twice. That felt like the wrong answer though, and he kept it vague. "Here and there."

"Are you able to get us electricity and meter readings?"

Toby nodded and Juliet smiled and got in the lift, pressing

the topmost button to the forty-eighth floor.

"Why the metre readings?" Tom quizzed once they were alone.

"I want to get a sense of how often he was here," Juliet replied. "Even a superhero uses electricity."

As the doors opened and Juliet walked into the flat, the sense of space she'd found in the lobby continued. Every room possessed a wall of glass, meaning the backdrop in every corner of the property was a skyline view of London stretching to the horizon. From bed you'd be able to see The Shard, The 'Walkie-Talkie' and the Thames with nothing blocking the view. Unable to help it, Juliet pictured herself waking up in the mornings, having coffee and breakfast out in the private garden. The property was another world.

Passing officers searching the place, Tom and Juliet moved from room to room steering clear of them. The bedroom was their first stop, a king-sized bed surrounded by two glass walls. The bathroom similarly made use of the light, which bounced off the marble walls and white surfaces. The feel of the place was very similar to a top-end hotel, not a speck of dirt anywhere, even the windows, and it was hard to picture someone living there full time.

"It doesn't look lived in," Juliet remarked as they left the bathroom.

"A place like this wouldn't," Tom replied, a level of bitterness in his voice. "If you can drop a few million pounds to live in a flat like this, having a cleaner multiple times a week, even daily, isn't a stretch."

"So where's his toothbrush?"

The question prompted a shared glance between Juliet and Tom; he turned a head back to look at the sink and while there were plenty of expensive toiletries, a toothbrush was nowhere in sight.

Into the kitchen, Juliet moved to prove her point further. Opening the fridge, she revealed it being completely bare.

"Not out the ordinary for a superhero that busy to not find time to do a food shop. Did he even need to eat?" Tom commented.

"He had to eat," Juliet scorned. "The point I was making was that if you have a cleaner, and live in a place like this, it's not beyond reason he'd pay to have food delivered and packed away for him. I don't see any longer-lasting products either. Even a superhero would have had a preferred condiment."

"Ketchup?" Tom queried.

"From the North East? I reckon a brown sauce kind of man," Juliet replied.

"Maybe he mostly ate out?"

"For every meal? If so, where?"

"What is it you're saying, Juliet?"

"I'm not saying a thing," Juliet replied. "Ethan asked us to keep an eye out for anything missing that you'd usually expect. We're in his home. Supposedly the one place on this entire planet where John Fitzgerald could rest his head or come for a break. I'm saying that this doesn't look much like a home, even for somebody who uses it fleetingly. No photos on the wall, no books, no personal bits and bobs. It feels like a showhome."

"Okay, so where to next?" Tom enquired. "Want to speak to a few of his neighbours?"

"The neighbours won't have seen him. He flew in from the sky most of the time. Didn't Toby mention a sky lounge with private dining facilities?"

"He did."

"Should we get him to show us?"

"I can't stand hearing any more of the company lines," Tom replied. "I'm sure we can find it ourselves."

Leaving Ethan's officers to photograph and look for anything of interest, Juliet and Tom headed out of the flat. The route to the sky lounge from the flat proved a bit of an adventure, down a floor in the lift, along a corridor and up a staircase. When they reached it, the place felt immediately like a collector's den. On every table, in most of the space, were objects like globes, binoculars, old books and antiques. In another environment Juliet would have them pinned as tacky imitations, but it was clear from the cost of the Invictus Building they'd be very much real.

There were groups of people dotted around, some reading the morning papers, some having an early breakfast. A member of staff's eyes flicked up from behind the bar and immediately glanced away. The contrast between the friendly, fake smiles Juliet had encountered so far grabbed her interest. Cautious in her style, Juliet chose not to make an approach right away, leading Tom on a long meander as they attempted to appear interested in their surroundings. The barmaid had something in her locker, all right. Her eyes continually flicked in their direction with a single sentence repeating in her mind: *Give nothing away.*

Finally, Juliet led the approach and without the need of her ability to mind-read, watched the body language of the barmaid tighten.

"Hi, we're hoping to speak to a few members of staff for a moment. What can I call you?"

"Elspeth."

"I'm Juliet," she said, taking a seat at the bar. "Have you

worked here long?"

"Over a year," the barmaid smiled.

"I'm not sure if you've heard, but I have questions about John Fitzgerald?"

A flicker in her face, but Elspeth did a magnificent job of concealing her thoughts. Juliet's power was less complex than others painted or presumed, sometimes in a way that played to her advantage. Juliet could not read the innermost details of anyone she wanted. Someone could sit her next to a murderer on a train for hours, but unless the person thought about their crimes, Juliet would remain oblivious to them. Continuing the example, the person could ponder one of their murders but Juliet would have no name, location or the visual image of what the person was thinking. The thoughts were like trying to witness the full complexity of a face-to-face conversation with a wall in the way. Without body language, they would lose tone and context, and the same idea worked for mind-reading.

"Ask away," Elspeth said with a tight smile. Instead of replying, Juliet waited and let the awkwardness build between them. The expression she painted on her face was quizzical, as if there was something that Juliet could infer from Elspeth's manner. The barmaid looked barely twenty, and carried herself with that same youthful nervousness – this was probably her first job out of school. A steady job with regular hours in a world where that was getting rarer. The residents liked consistency in the faces they interacted with. The tips were probably huge too. For Elspeth this represented a golden opportunity, one where she didn't want to breach the privacy of a resident, even if they were dead, for fear of recriminations. All those details Juliet could infer just from looking at Elspeth. Another key sentence repeated in her mind: *I can't take it.*

"What couldn't he take?"

The colour drained from Elspeth's face as Juliet asked the question. Acknowledging the recent thought was a simple power play to throw her off. It worked. As Elspeth stumbled and looked for an appropriate response, words and snippets leaked out from the memory. *John had sat at the bar, ordering more and more drinks until he was drunk. Other residents and staff noticed his condition, but none felt able to tell John he'd had enough.* I can't take it, *he kept murmuring to himself as he clutched a glass.* I can't take it.

"I don't know what you mean?" Elspeth replied with a play-acted frown to illustrate her confusion. A poor attempt at concealment, but Juliet had what she needed. The member of staff could also hold firm that she'd revealed none of the secrets or misdemeanours of a resident. Discretion and privacy was everything in an institution like this.

"I'll pretend like you had nothing to say," Juliet promised. "Just tell me how long ago that moment at the bar was. Did you see or hear anything like that before?"

Elspeth relaxed, her eyes flicking to Tom. "Around three weeks ago. I've worked at Invictus for over a year and it's the first time I ever saw John eat or drink in here. I knew he was a resident, he just kept himself to himself."

"Thank you for your help," Juliet replied as she slid off the stool.

"There was something else," Elspeth blurted out. As Juliet raised a brow, Elspeth flustered further. "A name, he would occasionally mutter it under his breath. The same one every time."

"Whose name?" Juliet challenged.

"Alice," Elspeth answered. "He kept saying the name Alice

under his breath."

Chapter Three

The crowds had thickened when Juliet and Tom exited the Invictus lobby. Half-past eight in the morning and school kids milled around in packs, and pairs of people huddled and pointed up to the penthouse. Their minds all said the same thing. *That's where John Fitzgerald lived.* Lived. Already John had slipped into the past tense.

In half an hour, the Prime Minister George Eden would make a statement revealing the truth to the world. Would a day of mourning follow? As Juliet glanced at the crowd's faces, there was an excitement and buzz in the air. The reality hadn't sunk in yet.

As Juliet walked to the car, a figure darted out from the crowd. Before she could even react, Tom put a firm hand on the man's shoulder, towering over his weedy frame.

"Is that Juliet Reynolds?" the man squeaked, startled.

"She might be," Tom cautioned, his arm remaining on the man. "What would it be to you?"

"I have information related to John Fitzgerald," he insisted. "I presume she's working the case?"

Tom and Juliet exchanged a glance. He was a small, scruffy-looking man who looked like he'd just got up and been dragged through a hedge backwards. Yet those who toed the line between conspiracy theorist and crucial informant often existed on the fringes of normal behaviour. The man appeared harmless enough, and his thoughts aligned to his words. Eager to spill the beans, his mind jumped from place to place with no sign of slowing. Juliet signalled to Tom that it was okay, who promptly let the man go.

"My name is Leo Turner, I'm a moderator on a website called Fitzgerald Watch," he gushed the moment Tom's hand left his shoulder. This man wanted an audience, any audience, and if Tom was there too, so be it. "We're a community dedicated to mapping out John's route around the globe, tracking the casualties saved and impacts in statistics John had. I've been a member for close to a decade, back from when we were a simple internet forum. I've been tracking him as a hobby ever since."

"Do you know where he was between last night and this morning?" Tom suggested, trying his luck.

"Well, that's the thing," Leo enthused. "If someone posts a selfie with John, we'll find it. If someone publishes a news story, regardless of language, it'll get translated and added to the site. When I say we have members all over the world, I mean it. Yet for the last two weeks he hasn't been seen in public. Not a sighting in the sky or a news story anywhere."

"And this place?"

"Part of the website is that we track his comings and goings on a map," Leo enthused. "Years ago we placed a tracking camera pointed at his balcony and one at the main entrance with a live feed through to our group page. Whatever that place is, it isn't John Fitzgerald's home. Two years ago he was here often, dropping in and out. John last popped in three weeks ago, his first visit in four months."

"That's expected though, isn't it?" Juliet questioned, her face doubtful. "The time John spent in war zones and helping with natural disasters, he'd have other boltholes to sleep in."

"So where are they?" Leo quizzed in retort, an enthusiastic smile returning to his face.

"I don't follow," Juliet began, but a mobile phone appeared in her hand before she could speak another word.

On the screen was a map, a filter to one side allowing the user to select their chosen time range. As Juliet selected the last six months, the map became a sea of red dots bouncing all over the globe. When she selected a longer time period, the red spread, each dot representing a sighting.

"Now select the last two weeks."

Juliet did so, and the map before her was absent of any red dots.

"I've been part of this community for over a decade, and for us to not know where he is... well, it's unprecedented. He's too famous a face to drop off the map."

"So where do you think he's been the past two weeks?"

"Held somewhere? A secret mission? That's your job to find out. But if you want to find out why someone murdered John, your answer will not be in a flat he's never lived in."

Silence fell and Juliet realised that Leo would happily remain with them, spilling the entire back catalogue of information he had on John Fitzgerald if she didn't move on. From her jacket she pulled out a business card, a simple square with her name and contact number. "Call me if anything that may help comes up, you've been so helpful."

Juliet watched Leo's chest swell with pride as he took and pocketed the card. Juliet's praise wasn't insincere as she walked away with Tom towards the car. History taught her that the more people out there gathering evidence Juliet could later tap into, the better her chance of uncovering something would be. The part of the investigations Juliet's scope covered was intelligence rather than any evidence that would appear in court. A man like Leo had more tacit knowledge of John Fitzgerald than most individuals alive.

"We're big fans of yours too," he said after her. "You're the last one!"

The sentence shuddered as it repeated in Juliet's mind. Even without her ability, she knew what would be in many people's minds. With John dead, that left Juliet as the sole British individual with an ability. Famous – how could you not be with an ability – Juliet usually caught people's attention in a room. Yet today the focus would become more intense. They reserved the mind-reader for police work and John, well, for everything else.

"Where to next?" Juliet asked, opening the car door. "Have you been in touch with Ethan?"

"He can spare us twenty minutes," Tom answered. "It's breakfast time and I'm craving a bacon roll and a coffee."

Ten minutes down the road and they found a place to accommodate their needs. As Tom queued for a food van serving builders and suited office workers alike, Juliet waited on a bench she'd nabbed. It was the beginning of summer, that sliver of time in the British calendar where the rain paused for a week or two, and the air tasted a note fresher than normal. The forecast was cloudless all day, and she imagined the pavements to be full come lunchtime as people attempted to escape the confinement of their workplaces for half an hour's sun. Juliet's prepared breakfast of choice was oats mixed with Greek yogurt and berries. Later on, as a snack, she had a bag of mixed nuts and an energy bar to see her through. Knowing when the next meal was coming proved a rarity in her occupation.

On her phone she flicked through the website Leo had referenced. The site held a bank of detail regarding recent movements. John could be in Vietnam one day, Slovakia the next, but mobile footage and local news stories would follow him every step of the way. Three weeks ago he'd been in India doing a United Nations poverty talk, then he was in Afghanistan helping pull people out of a landslide. Finally, there'd been a high school shooting in the US. John arrived too late to step in, however, and there was a viral live news video of a grieving mother verbally attacking him.

Carmen Snead, who had a daughter unaccounted for at the time, cut a ragged and distraught figure in the video. Hair scraped back into a ponytail, eyes raw red from tears, she began by screaming that nobody was giving her answers. While they said would find her daughter alive and well, the media trailed her like vultures, capturing every distraught moment. Wrong place, wrong time, John flew down from the sky only several yards away.

"Where were you?" Carmen screamed as Juliet scanned over the news footage. John's skin was covered in soot and his clothes were ripped and torn. There was confusion in his eyes as he tried to take in what was happening. But as Juliet paused the rolling footage, his face displayed more than confusion – he was exhausted. Another fire, another few lives to save, and a world where demand outmatched his supply.

Suddenly Carmen lunged forward, grabbing for John. Before she could make contact and escalate the situation, the crowd yanked the distraught mother into its clutches. In the brewing hysteria, they led John towards the school. By the time the footage had been taken, the teenager had already turned the gun on himself after murdering four fellow pupils and a teacher. The clip lasted less than thirty seconds, yet millions had replayed it around the world.

Tom returned balancing two coffees with a bacon roll. He spotted Juliet eating the oats out of her Tupperware.

"I don't know how you can eat that stuff every morning."

"It's good for you," Juliet bit back. "Better than all the fat in that bacon roll."

"Bacon's good for the soul," he said, handing over the coffee. "I got it how you like it. Two sugars and enough milk to make me sick."

"I'm not sure that bacon part is based on science."

"What do they know?" Tom concluded. "One week wine stops dementia, the next it causes heart disease. One week chocolate is good for you, one week it's bad."

Ignoring the coffee jibe, Juliet continued, "I'm not sure they've ever argued a daily bacon roll from whatever food van you can find is good for you."

"Well, maybe that should be their next study."

Juliet laughed, and Tom took a seat. Ten to nine. The prime minister was due to make his address in ten minutes. Despite John Fitzgerald's name trending on social media, scepticism and doubt filled many of the posts. As soon as he made the statement, the world would change.

"Where were you for the Cherwell School fire?" Juliet quizzed as they ate their food.

"Still on the beat," Tom replied with a mouthful. "I won't lie,

I missed most of what was happening. Before smart phones, it was only really when I clocked off and got home that the news shows were playing the footage. You?"

"Sixth-form," Juliet replied. "We all gathered round the computers and searched for any scrap of information. The days to follow, when they made the public reveal, was insane."

"Your powers would surely have developed by then?"

"They were emerging," Juliet acknowledged. "It'd be two more years before they developed fully. Seeing John in that footage, it took my breath away. By that point I could hear whispers from friends and teachers, what thoughts were ticking through their minds. I thought I was going insane. To see someone like John, to have a trailblazer mapping out the way for me... I'm not sure where I'd be without him."

"It'll be another world," Tom considered.

Spooning another mouthful of oats into her mouth, Juliet continued to eat. Relentless would be the word Juliet would use to describe the world, at least her part of it, before John died. Every day there was a fresh case, some crime that needed attention or a witness investigating. People presumed as Juliet and John were both British and had powers they knew each other well, yet both of them were far too busy for much interaction. Actors had Hollywood award ceremonies to bring them all into the same room outside of film sets, but there were no award shows for the superhumans like John and Juliet. When they crossed paths a handful of times, it could barely be called a shared glance. As Juliet ate, her mind flicked back to the footage of John being accosted at the school shooting. Only once in a while, a report a month, she got the sense that people were forgetting the human element of that title. Humans make mistakes. Humans have limitations. If people were expecting perfection, what would happen when they didn't get it? What would happen now the biggest one of them all was gone?

"It makes little sense," Juliet bemoaned. "None of it does."

"It's never made much sense," Tom replied.

The response threw Juliet slightly, and she looked over at her partner, deep in thought with a bacon roll in his hand. "A handful of individuals across the globe who can read minds, fly, deflect bullets or shoot fire out their hands. We've never got close to working out how your abilities work the way they do, why the people who possess them do. Yet somehow we'll try to figure out how John's powers stopped working. Any actual idea how you read minds?"

Juliet shook her head. "It's like a tap. Someone once twisted it to let the water flow, and it never stopped."

"So theoretically a stranger turning John's power off like that," Tom said, snapping his free fingers to illustrate, "is nonsense."

"The barmaid met him three weeks ago. He sat at her bar and drank himself into a state. Kept muttering to himself, '*I can't take it*'."

"Maybe he'd had a tough day, the kind that makes you reconsider things. Being a superhero like that is a tough paper-round."

"He's not the only one who feels that way," was the sentence Juliet wanted to say, but she noticed people all around her had stopped what they were doing, eyes glued to their phones. Juliet pulled hers out and shared the stream from the BBC app with Tom.

A podium waited empty in front of Downing Street, near the famous black door. The same spot where past Prime Ministers resigned or made statements of great importance to the world.

The ticker below stated that George Eden, the Prime Minister, would make an urgent address. As Juliet read it, she spotted the door swing open and the portly man in his mid-sixties stride out. A soft politician, the kind to take care of the numbers and fade into the background. The coming days would be the biggest of his career.

"Good morning, Britain. It is with great sadness that I stand here today to announce one of our fellow citizens, John Fitzgerald, has been found dead. His death is being investigated as a murder. The victim is one well known to every man, woman and child, both here and further afield. Hero, saviour, our champion and Superman, the loss today is unimaginable. What I can tell you so far is that, at five this morning, a member of the public stumbled upon John's body and our finest officers are chasing down leads as we speak. In the next hour, Gregg O'Connor, head of the Metropolitan Police, will hold a briefing and share what scant details we have.

"The news of John lying dead in our capital city, will fill all listening with disbelief, terrible sadness, and a quiet fury. This murderous act was not just an attack on John, but on everything he stood for. The brightest beacon of freedom, opportunity, safety and hope, the blood spilled today is an attempt to frighten those principles into timid retreat. I stand here before you to promise that his murder will not crumble this nation. We did not cower during the Blitz, the Great Fire or to any group who has tried to topple Great Britain. Today, our nation sees evil, the worst of human nature. And we will respond with our best. To those waking up to the news, scared of the uncertain future before us, I have no immediate answers. I can only tell you what my mother would say whenever I saw something I feared on the news. Look for the helpers. The police, the emergency services and the ordinary citizens checking on neighbours or providing calm with a simple cup of tea. Out there right now, there are so many people helping.

"As soon as the news reached me I implemented our government's emergency response plans. Our intelligence agencies, police force and military are both prepared and powerful, as too are those of our allies. The functions of our government continue without interruption. Our police remain steadfast in the face of this murder, protecting the citizens of this country and keeping us safe. The search is underway for those who are behind this evil act. I've directed the full resources of our intelligence and law enforcement communities to find those responsible and to bring them to justice. Britain has faced dark days before, and we will do so in the days to come. None of us will ever forget this day. Yet I promise we will catch John Fitzgerald's killer and we will bring those accountable to justice. Thank you."

"Our finest officers," Tom repeated, a smirk on his face. "I'll tell my mum about that one."

"No pressure," Juliet agreed. "Maybe we should get back to it? When the Prime Minister described the police force as both prepared and powerful, I don't think he meant you armed with a bacon roll."

"You should see me once I've had a full English breakfast," Tom said, a wry smile on his face. "No criminal is safe."

Dusting themselves down, Tom chucked his coffee cup and paper bag into the bin next to their bench as Juliet packed away her Tupperware into her rucksack.

"Are you going to be okay?" Tom asked, sincerity creeping into his voice.

"I'll be fine," Juliet stated. Tom didn't say it, but the name of Will Bowman entered his mind. The biggest case she'd ever worked before had now been eclipsed. "Murder cases get under my skin. What's happened before won't happen again."

Chapter Four

Hostility swirled around thousands of miners and police. Bottles, sticks and bricks hurtled in every direction while the crowd roared. For a few brief moments, the police on horseback appeared out of the sea of uniforms. The confrontation outside of the Bellington mining pit, beneath blue autumn skies, hid a dramatic, almost desperate air. There was a crush of bodies, pressing against lines of police shields as they tried to force their way through.

Among the swirling ruck of bodies trying to push against the line was a determined-looking man, relishing the brutal excitement of it all. Mike shouted and punched his way into the middle of a riotous battle with the cops. The intoxicating sounds of the violent crowd made his veins pulsate.

"COAL NOT DOLE," the large and angry crowd snarled with Mike at its centre. Ready to release his repressed rage against the establishment, a powerful fist waited, clenched at his side. A forbidding character with an intense stare, Mike stood unafraid of any battle. As the police with truncheons and shields moved in, Mike braced himself for the fight to come.

Mike had mattered then. When coal was still king, Bellington did too. The miner's strike had been a battle about pride, a way of life, the town's entire existence. They lost the battle and lost the war.

The dregs of a pint before him, Mike wondered where the time had gone. Where had the young man with impressive muscles disappeared to? Once he had torn through the crowd, dodging missiles and baton swipes. Now he could barely hobble to the pub and back in one piece.

After the coal went, Mike and Bellington continued to exist, even if the rest of the country liked to pretend they didn't. Working-class industries, working-class jobs, and working-class people. From steel to coal to shipbuilding, one by one the government came for them all. The scars remained, the child witnesses had become adults and eventually the wise old heads around town. An unmistakable sense of purpose remained stolen from them. Bellington was where you were born, where you'd die and everything you were. If Bellington was nothing but a forgotten scar, what was Mike?

"It was a dirty job, a dangerous job. But it was not demeaning," Mike would preach to anybody who would listen. "We loved working together, depending on each other. There was a sense of community that's not here today." The sentiment uttered a dozen times a day to other men who echoed the same sentiments in different words.

A bell rang from the bar, and an ache brewed in his chest. Eleven and last orders at the Rose and Crown. Dotted around the dated furnishing, several men either hauled themselves to their feet or remained satisfied with their last drink. On a Tuesday evening the faces, as much fixtures as the furnishings, all belonged to the old crowd. The ex-squaddies, miners or men who worked with their hands scattered among the tables and chairs. They would exchange words and conversations some nights, others none. That night, Mike opted to stew in his own thoughts in the corner as the pints consumed became countless.

With what only felt like a blink, the pub emptied as tired and hollow bar staff called time on another evening's ritual. Mike stood in the doorway with another patron, smoked a cigarette before exchanging a nodded goodbye.

In the distance, beyond the old miners' cottages, row upon row, would be the two old pitheads. All coalmines had to have two, for safety reasons. Catch them at the right time and Bellington's stood silhouetted against the metal Northumberland sky. A backdrop for a lifetime.

Time passed.

Mike's mouth, dry and gasping, demanded attention. His hand grasped for a glass of water on the bedside and found there was not one. Empty food wrappers, receipts and a load of other crap was all that his hand could find for company. The resolve to haul himself to his feet and start the arduous task of finding both a glass and the tap would be some time coming. A self-loathing fire needed feeding first.

As Mike peeled the initial layer of the day back, the cogs in his head pounded and reluctantly turned. Where had he been the night before? How much poison had he drilled into his fracturing body? What embarrassing act or statement would come back to humiliate him later? Alone in his twisted sheets, the anxieties needed boxing away, emotions to be caged and buried. The layers between sleep and consciousness were plentiful, not an instant switch from one to the other. His feverish nightly dreams were still too fresh to be comfortable.

There had been a maze, a concrete one too high to see

over. Running from something but finding no exit, Mike had awoken regularly in a cold sweat only to be hauled back into the darkness and terror. The maze was one of the regular dreams. The drink always found comfort in pulling the strings of delicate fears and horrors. Sometimes the walls would move in, squeezing his chest and body, trapped until he awoke with wheezing and heavy breath. The line between dream and waking was never clear-cut. Sometimes the man or people chasing him were physically at the foot of his bed before his eyes. Blinking their shapes and revulsion away could take minutes.

Mike knew he was dying. He could taste it, metallic in his sticky, condemned mouth. Pulling himself to his feet, he kicked clothes, clutter and all manner of mess out of his way en route to the bathroom. There he pissed mustard urine and looked down to see blood in the toilet bowl. A scan of the mirror illustrated a man staring back with a raw red nose and haunted yellow eyes. The decade-long lie that the colour was just the result of nicotine.

A headache throbbing, Mike stumbled to the shower and hauled himself under a stream of warm water. The heat brought his grumpy, reluctant body to attention. A single voice in the back of his mind begged for Mike to return to the duvet covers. *Sleep, curl up in comfort. You have nothing to get up for, anyway.*

Some days that little voice would win and Mike would sleep the day away. Such a choice was never worth it. The longer he slept, the longer he stayed awake. Routine was the only thing that kept Mike somewhat sane. Later that day he would recall with bitterness the moments spent emerging from his slumber in the shower. If only he had crawled back into bed for more rest. Then, at least, there was a fraction of a chance he'd never have woken up at all.

Instead, Mike pulled on a shirt and a pair of tracksuit bottoms. He muttered a meek promise to wash more clothes that day under his breath, fooling nobody. He owned no washing gel, powder or even a functioning machine to clean them. The damp smell of decay lingered in jackets, blankets, every pore on his body. A damp, musty corruption that had stretched over himself without retreat long ago.

The kettle boiling, Mike winced at the noise and pulled the least-dirty cup he could find from the side. A finger and some water cleaned it well enough. When he hunted for remaining contents in coffee jars, every one came up empty. With no food in either, Mike swore and went rooting through drawers and the pockets of clothes until finally he discovered a crumpled note.

On his way to the corner shop, no sense of day or time, it surprised Mike to see so many faces around the place. He dismissed it as a weekend or school holidays. Groggy and half-asleep, he slid past all the huddles and into the shop. A jar of instant coffee, tins of Special Brew and a sliced loaf. Mike made no excuses anymore to the server. They could see all they needed to know before them. A barely surviving alcoholic, best just to serve him and let him be on his way. Today proved strange, however – Mike had to get the shopkeeper's attention and struggled to maintain it. His eyes were fixed to some video playing on his phone and wordlessly they exchanged money and goods. With the change pocketed, Mike thought no more of it on his way back to the most hopeless and loneliest home he'd even known. The wife? Dead. The first-born son? Dead. The other son? Fuck knows where. Life passed by at this stage.

It surprised Mike he'd made it as long as he had.

Clearing a space on the sofa, Mike bundled two slices of bread into his mouth to soak up the bile and nastiness in his stomach. By this point daytime television would be on, maybe even Jeremy Kyle. Hopefully, there'd be a brawl. Mike liked it when the guests brawled.

Then Mike saw it, the pictures. Instinct made him flick the channel, but it was no use. Every channel, every transmission pumping out the same coverage from the same news stations. The face of his son, archive footage of him flying in the sky, putting out fires. His throat closed, his head spun, and Mike reluctantly turned up the volume. The newsreader wearing a black suit and a black tie, his words deliberately sober and expression grave.

"We regret to inform you this morning that a member of the public discovered John Fitzgerald's body in London. Police are treating the situation as a murder..."

Is that what the headline said? Mike's head flicked back to dreams of the maze and feverish hallucinations. Could it be real? His stomach aching and churning, the words continued in a similar vein on every channel he flicked to. Every time he got closer to listen. Something about a stabbing, multiple wounds. The Prime Minister made a statement.

Mike's hands shook. His son. Jonathan.

There was no being sober for this, he thought, every part of his body shutting down and looking for its crutch.

A tremor took over as he opened a can.

Chapter Five

A Londoner most of her adult life, Juliet knew rush hour in the capital city well. Twice a day Tube stations swelled with people, roads halted and pavements became a blurred chaos of under and over-taking. Anarchy gripped the city, yet gradually it'd untangle itself and order would resume. The hour following the announcement of John's murder was something else entirely.

In the car's safety, halted in traffic, Juliet listened to the thoughts that filtered into her mind. All focused on the murder, attempting to digest and make sense of it. Glued to smartphone screens, Juliet watched strangers shake their heads and mutter statements of disbelief to each other. Only in tragedy would Londoners break the sacred code of silence among strangers. The disbelief and immediate anxiety that filled their minds was identical to Juliet's own shock a couple of hours earlier.

Even with the Prime Minister's announcement, many doubted whether the information could be true. Others speculated the death of John Fitzgerald could only be an assassination at the hands of a foreign nation. Yet why would any kill him, on foreign soil in such a sloppy manner? The tension building inside people's minds showed a failure to internalise the situation. To those Juliet witnessed and heard, the news didn't feel like the murder of an individual; it felt like an attack on a way of life. John Fitzgerald was as known to children as their own family members. Imagining a life or country without John was like imagining the Queen dying, yet somehow more shocking to the core. The Queen had a successor, an institution built around her, whereas John Fitzgerald wasn't *meant* to die.

Tom and Juliet's driver tried to pass throngs of people with no obvious purpose. There seemed no time for work or reality as the world stood still for something closer to fiction. Disbelief could easily swell in hysteria. Surely it was only a matter of time before the Prime Minister announced formal days of mourning? The monarch would receive such treatment, so why not the country's home-grown superhero?

Somebody out there had enough access to the most powerful man alive to catch him off-guard. The murderer knew of a way to disable John's well-known regenerative abilities. With the superhero out of the way, would there be a follow-up? A further attack? From the car window Juliet's eyes fell on troops and armed police outside Tube stations, a signal of security and safety. The Prime Minister had felt the need to make that decision, the type made in the event of a terrorist attack. London was a city under an invisible siege, against an unknown enemy.

"How are the kids?" Juliet asked to break the silence of twenty minutes in the car. The driver's instructions were to take them to the base of operations.

"I told my wife something big had happened, and she's keeping them off school today. They're too young to understand, but they'll pick up on any atmosphere. Better to let them play," Tom said.

The Specialist Crime and Operations Directorate's Homicide Command, a name which had taken years for Juliet to memorise, undertook all homicide investigations in London. Split geographically into six units, Ethan's branch was East London. Inside the building the entire investigation would take place, from autopsy to interviews. As the driver pulled up outside, armed police covered every angle and exit.

"They've moved the body inside," Juliet stated with certainty.

They checked Juliet and Tom's identification passes at least three times on the way in. Nobody was getting in or out of the command centre who wasn't supposed to be there. Inside there was hustle and bustle, officers pacing and making rapid phone calls. Their name badges stated many government agencies and positions. From police to civil service to intelligence agency personnel, there was a sense of chaos, urgency and getting stuff done. Their minds were unruly and untamed. Juliet couldn't help but sneak in here and there. Spies in terrorist circles had nothing, plants in foreign agencies had nothing. Every tip, every informant, and every semblance of a lead was coming up blank. They all had *nothing*.

"Let me find Ethan," Tom instructed as they paused in a waiting room. "I'll see where we're at with the investigation."

As Juliet sat, she gazed upon a room full of discarded coats, breakfast sandwich wrappers, empty coffee cups and deserted seats. The room stank and was stuffy, and Juliet reasoned that many of the people she'd passed on the way had been here since the early hours. A break for the next few days was unthinkable.

The only animation in the room came from a small muted

television screen in the corner playing BBC News. The headline was obvious, but over the inaudible newsreaders was the incredible footage taken for granted for so many years. A montage of heroic snippets: John pulling bodies out of burning buildings, to hauling gasping citizens from flood waters. The images were like a comic book movie brought to life, almost clichéd, but showed the grounded, gritty work the superhero did day to day. No aliens, super-villains, or valiant battles. Like chores, the footage was John's nine to five routine.

Then, on the television screen before Juliet, the most iconic footage appeared: John's first act of heroism, the Cherwell School fire. In an era of drones and worldwide smartphone usage, it would surprise many to cast their mind back to 2006. Mobile phones had cameras that could record only a minute's grainy footage at a time. On the television screens in front of Juliet, the infamous mobile phone footage of the school on fire played; the tennis courts outside swarming with pupils and smoke billowing out of the third floor. The audio was jagged, loud, and with a lot of interference. As the footage rocked and bounced, the viewer could just about make out the situation. School children wildly looked upon their school on fire. Firefighters had joined the chaos, their attention fixed higher. Trapped on the fourth floor, above the flames, was a classroom full of children.

Juliet recalled the silence and concern as she'd first watched the video all those years ago. How could the firefighters rescue all those pupils in time? The mood of the clip calmed as the weight of the situation dawned on the cameraman. There was a class full of children trapped and about to burn to death before their eyes.

At this point the footage cut away, presumably hitting the

end of the phone's storage capabilities. The next video was further away, a hiding child commentating. The crowd was cheering, jumping, and it was unclear what was happening. For less than ten seconds the video focused on a pixilated figure flying down from the air, grabbing a falling child and floating to the ground. The child placed into the safe arms of emergency services.

The video then switched, another phone and another angle. The extraordinary footage continued as the figure flew into the air, now grabbing two at a time in each arm. Juliet and her friends in sixth form had looked at each other questioningly and the person on the computer dutifully pulled up the accompanying news articles stating every child survived the fire. Some articles referred to the unverified video, but many did not. The first question was obvious. Was it real or was it fake?

Today the world recognised the figure in the footage as John Fitzgerald, a soldier on leave from duty in the right place at the right time. As Juliet's mind drifted from the footage on the news channel, she dwelled on the Cherwell School fire. How often could humanity witness a story where everything turned out okay? A story where the ordinary man wins and nobody suffered? The hope that filled the country that day was unlike anything Juliet had ever encountered. The world had its own protector. Now he lay dead in another room.

"The body is ready," Tom said as he poked his head around the corner.

Getting up from her seat, Juliet followed Tom as he led her through corridors and down several staircases. The room he took her to was a morgue and a team of doctors stood patiently over a sheet covering the body. Of varying ages, Juliet paid little attention to them as the lump of John's body lay before her. The surreal experience captivated her attention until a figure to her right spoke.

"Any luck with any of the neighbours and staff?"

Juliet traced the voice back to Ethan. It had only been a few hours since they last spoke, yet the stress looked visible on his face. Still, he managed a faint smile.

"The staff barely had any interaction with him bar an incident three weeks ago. The flat looked like a showroom: no personal possessions, toiletries or food. What we saw wasn't where John Fitzgerald lived."

"You have been busy," Ethan smiled, though the negative news registered in both his face and mind. The news that John lived elsewhere was another complication in the case. "What was the incident three weeks ago?"

"John went to the bar in the building, and got so drunk that he could barely stand. Was muttering about not being able to take it."

"Take what?"

"Your guess is as good as mine," Juliet concluded. "Plus, he's been missing for two weeks."

"Who did you hear that from?"

"A man named Leo runs a website dedicated to tracking John Fitzgerald's movements. There's been no public sightings for nearly a fortnight."

"Christ," Ethan said. "Any good news?"

Tom and Juliet exchanged a glance. "I guess that depends on what you've got here."

"I'll hand that one over to you," Ethan sighed as he raised a hand toward the nearest doctor.

With straw-like ginger hair and bags under her eyes, there

was a sense of hostility in her. "Dr. Summers," she said, introducing herself. "As I was just saying to Ethan, I've begun the autopsy. This kind of thing takes a few hours, and you've given me less than one. Don't quote me on any hard conclusions. But so far the blood and initial findings are painting quite the picture."

"More good news?" Tom asked.

"Where to start," she stated. "Multiple stab wounds, over forty. Blood work has come back with traces of heroin in the system, yet nothing obvious to show why his regenerative abilities switched off. Further to that, we found things not conforming to previous medical examinations of him. There's a tattoo on his chest and scarring predating the cause of death. That's just what we have so far."

Juliet could read no lie in Dr. Summers' expression or thoughts. All truth.

"Could the heroin have switched off his ability?"

"Not from what we've seen so far. The quantities in his system, to put it crudely, would be enough to kill an elephant, but an analysis of his kidneys and liver shows no damage. His body regenerated after his last consummation of the drug," Dr. Summers said. Her feet were shuffling. Other doctors in the room pretended to be busy. Revealing the golden boy superhero had enormous volumes of one of the most dangerous drugs possible in his system wasn't how they'd pictured their morning.

"That's why we brought you in," Ethan stated. "In the hours leading to his death, John consumed significant quantities of heroin. A brief time later, someone murdered him. If we're trying to establish a timeline, this is it."

"So you're telling me that John Fitzgerald was a drug addict,"

Juliet said, growing flustered.

"I'm saying that John Fitzgerald had a cocktail of illegal drugs in his system upon his death, and depending on volume they could have been there as long as three days," Dr. Summer replied. "With such an extraordinary patient, and how his regenerative abilities functioned remaining largely a mystery, I can't accurately put a time on it."

"You mentioned a tattoo and scarring," Tom chimed in. "What did you mean by that?"

"On the previous medical reports there's no mention of the scarring or tattoo. From what I've been able to see so far, they aren't fresh. They're what any good doctor would reference."

"So John has had past injuries, inconsistent with the records," Tom stated bluntly. "No wonder they didn't want knowledge that someone could harm him out in the open. Who oversaw the previous medical examinations?"

"Dr. Walters," was Ethan's answer. "We've been trying to get in touch. He's a private doctor for the intelligence service. So far the commissioner is playing political football with the intelligence agencies to get an interview."

"So we have a victim whose whereabouts were unknown for two weeks. We don't know his real home address and in recent days he had a jolly with some heroin," Juliet said aloud.

"In addition, this high profile and immensely popular victim's murder is drawing more attention than any other case in recent memory," Ethan added. "The chief of police himself is due to make a statement later this morning. All we can give him is that John's abilities were probably exaggerated; we don't know where the hell he's been the last two weeks and, to top it off, he may or may not have been a drug addict."

"We don't know that," Tom responded, trying to cool the

room. "There may be more to it or further explanations."

"It's not like heroin is something you casually do one time," Juliet countered. "The needles, the technique, and even getting hold of the stuff in the first place needs a level of knowledge. This won't be John's first time."

"Maybe he was injected against his will, to keep him delirious?"

"Both could be right assumptions," Ethan relented. "Either way gives us a start of finding out where he may have been in the days or hours before his death. When the time comes that we get a hold of this Dr. Walters, I'm sure we'll learn the truth about his abilities. What about the tattoo?"

Pulling back the sheet, Dr. Summers revealed a dead John Fitzgerald to the room. His body pale sliced to pieces. It was difficult to see the old scarring but using a scalpel Dr. Summers talked them through it, showing the previous wounds beneath the fresh ones. She also pointed out the damaged skin of a tattoo. On John's chest there was a date: 05.05.2010.

"Six years ago," Tom stated.

"True," Juliet agreed. "I saw online he has a dead mother and brother. Could it relate?"

Tom did the sums in his head. "They died before Cherwell. A few years after both, I reckon. What can you tell about the existing scars?"

Dr Summers peeled back the covers further. "We have the fresh wounds leading to his death, but underneath there are older scars, burns and stab wounds. I can't date them, but they're not fresh. It's workable they came before his powers kicked in in the army, but they're significant and not noted in his records, which include the military days. The recent tattoo also disrupts that theory. All we really know about the onset of abilities is their frequent emergence in times of immense trauma. Wounds after John's development should have regenerated. Anything before would be on record."

The soldier who saved the schoolchildren, the best of Britain. After the Cherwell School fire, there was worldwide media attention. For weeks nobody talked about anything else. John Fitzgerald was unveiled at a press conference, and the UK government revealed to the world what had been going on behind the scenes.

The scientists could track the first case of a human being displaying abnormal abilities as far back as the eighties. During this time there was little more to the powers than seeing them as neat tricks. Telekinetic ability to move a pencil by a centimetre, or somebody able to heal from injuries in days that should have taken weeks. At this early stage there were no globally reaching press conferences. The anecdotal powers drew little media attention or government interest past a local level.

The situation changed at the turn of the millennium. Within the intelligence agencies, the situation escalated to something noteworthy. A boy, Marco Rossi, created a small fire playing in his room. A schoolgirl reported by her father as being able to read minds. Across the globe, a handful of people were popping up with unique abilities with their powers verging on dangerous. The intelligence agencies recruited those coming forward. Non-disclosure agreements and court super-injunctions blocking the reporting or wider revelation of these emerging individuals were put in place.

With the growing emergence of such gifted people, the government decided they could analyse the phenomenon in existing intelligence agencies and circles, and the humans blessed with such unique talents would be put to good use. Britain gathered a handful of talented people from all over Europe and Juliet had been one of them – the schoolgirl turned into the government by her own father.

"Partial prints on the bottle," Ethan acknowledged, bringing Juliet back into the room. Ethan and Tom had been continuing to bounce facts and ideas off each other as her focus drifted. "They're not complete enough to give us a match, even if we have them registered on the system. Although it'll give us a head start on any suspect we bring in."

"Plus the lack of gloves indicates this wasn't a professional hit."

"There's a footprint in the blood too."

"These are strong starting points," Tom said. "We getting anywhere on the CCTV footage or patrons of the nearby pub?"

"I'd like if you could speak to the owner and the regulars. Most are being interviewed upstairs by my team. The owner has been in touch with police this last week himself. Someone dented a padlock on his gate something rotten late last week, looked like they were trying to smash it, and gave up. A few businesses have had petty break-ins in the last few months. Seems like it's become a slight hot spot for drug addicts to make petty robberies they can pawn," Ethan answered. "My team has got hold of a lot of the CCTV from business owners, more than happy to help – they're combing through the last twenty-four hours to track comings and goings. It'll take a few hours to compile, but I'm certain one of them will have picked something up. Unless we're dealing with an invisible killer."

"I wouldn't even joke," Juliet chided. "The way this morning has gone already, I wouldn't rule it out."

Chapter Six

"Mr. Fitzgerald," a voice broke through the concrete maze. "Mr. Fitzgerald, are you okay?"

Eyes blinking into life, Mike stared at the police officer shaking him, another at the foot of his bed. The day, time and reality of the situation were all unclear. The charity of a drink was that it striped away memory. Mike forgot the last hour of a night, a name, where he lost his keys, and as life slipped away he had forgotten more than he remembered. Images remained, but they were only fragments; torn photographs only telling part of a story. Why were two police officers in his house? Anxieties jumped from one conclusion to the other, but before Mike could do much more he was rolling out of bed and past the officers into the bathroom.

Slumping onto the floor, Mike heaved bitter, metallic bile into the toilet bowl. Head spinning and ribs aching, he felt like someone had beaten him up. Had they? No, images of the television screen came flooding back and Mike realised it was not all a feverish dream. Looking over at him, with pitying eyes and an equal measure of both revulsion and concern, Mike had no time to apologise to the officers. The ritual was painful, foul and humiliating, but as Mike sat with his head spinning and sweat covering his face, he knew he was long past the point of shame.

One officer handed Mike a glass of water, which he swallowed before it came straight back up and into the toilet bowl. The officer gratefully grabbed the glass and went to get more water. Any excuse to get away from the bathroom.

The other, less timid officer, spoke. "Mr. Fitzgerald, it's about your son…"

Mike momentarily met the officer's eyes and an unspoken conversation confirmed that he already knew the required information. Mike hated the police. A long and heavy resentment that had never quite gone away. Back in the day while working in the pit and the strikes that came after, Mike had raged against brutal, tough men in uniforms with batons. Times had changed, the police were meant to be a friend now, but the uniform still instilled distrust.

Officer number one returned with water and this time Mike could keep it down, although he remained hugging the toilet bowl. This one had pity, tried to ignore the rotten smell and decay of the property she was in and the state of the man before her. Mike knew the thoughts going through their heads. *This was John Fitzgerald's father? The hero who could fly, move objects with his mind and deflect bullets? How had he come from this?*

"We're here to take you to London. They have the body, which needs identifying, and tests and interviews need to take place."

"How did it happen?"

"We don't know."

"Who did it?"

"We don't know."

"So what do you know?"

"As soon as you're ready, though our instructions are as soon as possible, we need you to pack a bag. You'll probably be staying a few days so take anything you might need," the officer paused, obvious that Mike had no clean clothes or even a bag. "I can ask somebody to clean up the place while you're gone?"

"They'll need a skip," Mike wanted to say. Instead he stayed silent, feeling enough of an inconvenience already.

Mike put what looked to be the cleanest clothes he owned in a plastic bin bag and sat in the back of a police car. In some anonymous car park, Mike said goodbye to the two officers, gave them his keys and moved into a far fancier car with his own personal driver. A Mercedes with plush seats and a crystal glass alcohol set, Mike went to help himself and steady his nerves. They had emptied the alcohol. The driver barely caught his eye the entire way to London, unclear whether to extend professional or personal courtesy. This suited Mike just fine.

At some point or another Mike drifted into a dream, a heavy alcohol-induced experience with vivid sights and sounds. In it two boys, who never turned to reveal their faces, kept running away inside the concrete maze. Mike would chase them, lose sight of them in a panic, only to spot them again at the edge of his vision. Frantically, he chased after the children, yelling as hard as he could with no sound escaping. The two children laughed, skipped and played until Mike could finally see neither at all.

Awake again, Mike had no sense of time. A sudden shuddering deep from within his stomach sent him sprawling to the floor of the car. The contents of his body long since emptied, only retching remained as sweat poured from his face.

In that moment decades flashed by: the day John was born, two boys playing with a ball in the street and rapidly, incoherently chatting about a film. There was bath time, stories and excited faces on Christmas Day. But there were also tears, pain and hurt.

There was once a time when Mike had come home to witness a scene in his front room. Maggie and a friend were playing with the boys – David, the older of the two, barely able to walk at that stage. Slathered in makeup, wearing a pair of his mother's red heels with a glittery pair of shades, David was happily toddling about the place to everyone's amusement. As Mike surveyed the scene, his oldest boy in drag and two grown women enjoying the spectacle, a dull rage filled him.

Mike didn't utter a word, pulling a beer out of the fridge and taking a seat in the corner as he watched. Maggie, the sweet obedient wife, picked up on the atmosphere her oblivious friend didn't. Calm in the corner, Mike's eyes never left his wife, who blushed and tried not to meet his gaze.

"I think it's probably time for me to get the boys cleaned up and down for a nap," Maggie whispered to the friend.

The friend offered help, Maggie rejected it, and within five minutes the family was once again alone. Maggie immediately turned, a realisation dawning along with a guilty voice. Mike hadn't even left his seat, hadn't even said a word, and Maggie was already apologising. Clear leadership was discipline and control.

Before a second more of begging could fill the room, Mike was on his feet, the back of his right hand smacking hard against her face. The world seemed to pause for a moment after he made the connection. Maggie's hand pulled to cover her face. "Mike, you hit me," she mumbled in shock.

Mike loomed over Maggie, fist now relaxed by his side. Down on the floor John was oblivious while David looked up at his parents, trying to make sense of the situation. What he learnt was that everything in life needed an authority, a mechanism to bring it back under control. In a company there needed to be a boss; a family also demanded a leader. Without it, Mike's family would be chaos.

"It was fun Mike," she had tried to say but his voice overruled her.

"If we had it your way, I'd be raising a pair of poofs," Mike spat. Her eyes were crying silently, her makeup running down her face. "Go clean yourself up, the boys don't need to see you in such a state."

The memory was neither the start of it nor the end, just a random point in-between. Like everything Mike came into contact with, the marriage wilted and festered. It failed not because there was nothing worth staying for; they had two lovely young boys and a comfortable home, but because there was no prospect for it to become anything worth having. At the time Mike did not see it but he did now; he'd dropped the reins even then. It was never a case of needing to be drunk all the time, rather Mike could not handle being sober. Every day his compass needed a drink to remain steady. The social camouflage of a friendship group based around booze hid it well, but that did nothing to slow the decay behind the scenes. No matter how much he tightened the grip, tried to keep in control, the foundations were crumbling.

The driver had permitted one stop, Mike grabbing a pack of cigarettes that the driver covered and a coffee from a service station chain. He offered one of the death sticks to the driver, a heavy-set man with a stern face who shook his head. Mike considered an attempt at a conversation as the man waited with him, but nothing was forthcoming, and Mike suspected the driver was there more as an escort than if he'd been left to his own devices on a random mode of public transport.

Concrete buildings, traffic and noise eventually replaced the sights of motorways and countryside. Mike had been to the capital before. Maggie thought it was important for the boys to see London, experience how different it was to Northumberland. The photos made the trip look like a pleasant one, smiling faces and two young beaming faces with ice creams. Behind the scenes Mike had been on edge the entire time – accents, places and people he had no anchor to. Drink, a steady flow, had once again been the only way he had got through. Initially, he remembered the trip well, but as the buildings moved by Mike in a blur, it was only those with photos he recalled.

"Mr. Fitzgerald," a sympathetic smile and voice greeted Mike as he stepped out of the car. "My name's Charlotte Taylor, I'm the police family liaison officer. First, I'd like to say how sorry I am about John. He was a lovely man and will be greatly missed."

"Thank you," Mike responded out of courtesy.

"I'll be your point of contact today. Anything you need, please just let me know," Charlotte continued. "I know it won't mean much considering the circumstance but… anything you need and I'll get right on it. You must be tired from the journey – would you like a coffee or some food?"

"Both would be lifesavers," Mike said, forcing a smile.

Charlotte, pretty for a police officer, did most of the talking as she gave fragmented snippets of information and drivel as they walked. She was obviously a 'people person' – Mike never knew how they did it. Once someone had said it became easier with age, but in every room and every conversation, Mike felt awkward and ill-fitting. The only social lubricant was the alcohol. Yet here was a young woman barely out of school who had mastered all the social rules without even a pause for thought.

The labyrinth of corridors seemed endless, dozens of men and women in suits all having hushed conversations or tapping away on phones. Regularly many would stop, look quizzically at Mike and Charlotte, and return to what they were up to. The comfy clothes Mike had picked suddenly felt like an uncomfortable skin. This wasn't his world. Offices, emails and soft accents.

The only respite came when Charlotte took Mike to his own kitchen, away from prying eyes. A bacon butty materialised from somewhere alongside a cheap coffee. Mike asked for brown sauce, but the utter look of confusion on Charlotte's face told him that there was no point repeating himself. Ketchup would do just fine. She left him to it and went to go find an aspirin.

The weight of the situation became plainer by the second. Mike never thought he'd be in a position where he was burying a son, let alone John. The death of parents is something every person grows up knowing as a necessary ending, but the reverse is far more crippling. Old, content and at peace with their history, Mike's heart would still sometimes long for his parents' company and wisdom but could accept the reality. The natural order of things was for the new to replace the old, and someday the night would draw in for himself too.

Painful but acceptable. Then the sickness came for David, his eldest son. That was the silver bullet and the death of it all. No parents, siblings and with a dead son, Mike only had bitterness and John left. Often they were the same thing in his eyes.

Mike considered an attempt to reconcile at one point – what a disaster that would have been. A coffee round at Mike's house, the milk sour and the place a tip as he mixed up the days? A conversation drier than the out-of-date biscuits provided. The idea had been sweet in his mind; father and son rebuilding bridges damaged years before. But what was there to rebuild? The old man staring at his child would know nothing of what stirred within. The child, now a man who stared back, never understanding the figure who raised him. A decade of false promises. Still, Mike never quite imagined they'd meet again like this.

It was Mike's fault; he was the father, and the supposed figure of experience, but that was part of the lie, wasn't it? In the eyes of children their parents are all knowing, all seeing beings, but really every adult is as shit-scared as the balls of flesh they're raising. They've just learnt to hide it better. The boys never saw the subtle phrases, hopes and dreams of their parents' arguments. Nor could they understand that their father was just as fragile as they were. How the fuck was Mike meant to cope with a dead wife and then a dead son in David? How did the boy ever have a chance?

Mike lit a cigarette and puffed. Old memories were stirring. He hated it. Too much time spent in the past and memories only made things worse. Television was his usual distraction, but the fuckers had stolen that possibility too. Instead, he sat penned in a tiny side kitchen somewhere, with either conversations about his son or memories of his son for company. The treat for dessert would be to see John's body.

"You can't smoke in here, Mr. Fitzgerald," Charlotte admonished as she re-entered.

"Where can I smoke?"

"Outside," Charlotte replied, her eyes wide as he took another drag. "The body, it's... they're ready to see you now."

Mike sighed and stubbed his cigarette out on the table. A look of horror passed over Charlotte's face, her concerned eyes never left the ash and remaining remnants of the cigarette on the table.

"Don't worry about it, I'm ready if they are," he said, the lie convincing nobody.

Hauling himself to his feet, the room suddenly felt unsteady and as he followed Charlotte, his steps were arduous. Every face they passed felt like they had eyes trained on Mike, and the temperature of the air dialled up a few degrees. Face red and sweating, Mike felt his hands shaking as he approached what looked to be the door.

"I'll be right outside," Charlotte smiled as she pressed the door open. "Take as long as you need."

Momentarily Mike's eyes flicked from the young lady to the beckoning room. Even with a body pumped full of booze, he never felt less numb than in that moment. Shoulders heavy and stomach feeling light, he let the door swing shut and approached the room. A waiting doctor stood on guard, face emotionless and mouth covered, but Mike had little time to stare at them. Everything seemed to orbit around the human-shaped figure covered by the sheet.

The doctor pulled back the sheet. Nothing could have prepared Mike for the reality of the scene before him. His son, dead on the table. There was no more to it.

"THAT'S MY BOY," bellowed as Mike's knees crumpled before the body.

The tears didn't feel thick enough. The crack in his voice or the shake of his core felt too weak. As Mike's hand fumbled for his son's hands, his entire body recoiled when he found them cold. The emotion was overbearing, Mike could not bring himself to look at the face of his son twice. Seeing him once would be enough for a lifetime.

Thoughts rushed back to the night John left. Or was it morning? The memory had twisted and revolved in Mike's own mind over the years. Drunk, so drunk he'd staggered to the sofa. Was that a night he'd pissed himself or vomited down his clothes? Time had blurred such facts.

The boy, good as gold, was trying to help get him off to bed, but the venom was thick that night. Dull rage clawing at any kind of reaction to feed itself. The words Mike wished he'd remembered but, like most things, had evaporated. Whatever was said, one line of poison had worked and it had crushed the last ounce of hope from the boy. Mike remembered the sadness, devastating disappointment and brewing anger frothing in the boy's eyes. That was unforgettable. The next morning John had gone, and it stayed that way the next day and a thousand days after that.

Then there had been the fire at Cherwell School years later. Mike hadn't caught the news that day. The fanfare passed him by completely in the bottom of a bottle. There was footage he'd see later, a press conference, interviews and photo shoots, but it was a while until Mike's eyes fell on the face of his son once more. The idea of superheroes living among them was straight out of the cartoons he'd raged so hard against the boys watching. That was until his face scanned a front page, saw his son front and centre. Mike begged the shopkeeper to read him every word of the article. When the truth became a reality, Mike snatched up the paper and would spend days going back to it. The boy had been okay; the boy had done all right. Undeserved and unearned pride welled up inside him.

One last look at the table and Mike's eyes welled up once more. His handsome boy, thick brown hair, a tattoo and a firm jaw he longed for. Someone he barely knew. John looked more like Maggie than Mike, and the memory of his lost family nauseated him. Before he left the room, embarrassed in his own company, Mike slapped his face twice, the sting focusing the pain somewhere physical. *Men don't cry.* Wiping away any tears, Mike greeted Charlotte with a stiff smile.

Chapter Seven

"Sometimes you have to let things play out the wrong way to let the course correct itself," Tom assured Juliet outside. She was pacing back and forth in a corridor after two hours in an interview room with various patrons of the Old Red Lion, the pub next to the crime scene.

"You have a person who can read minds and you stick her in a room with Dale who wants to rant about the immigration problem in Tower Hamlets, rather than anything to do with the murder," Juliet recounted wide-eyed, before slipping into an impression. "I bet it was one of *them*."

"So we can rule out any of the regulars or anybody inside the pub," Tom said, optimistic in his tone. "You spoke to all three of the people there until closing time. Nobody drank any wine that night. That closes one line of investigation."

"We're miles from solving this case."

"We have partial prints, footprints, and CCTV still to come," Tom said hopefully. "We've worked cases where we'd beg for that sliver of evidence."

"And what about the heroin, the scarring or fact that John didn't regenerate? Those answers aren't bits of information you find in a drawer somewhere. It's personal history, years of memories and stories. In an entire morning, not one person who was close to John Fitzgerald has come forward."

"The father is sitting upstairs."

"And from what you've told me, he hadn't spoken to John for over a decade," Juliet lamented. "Where did John Fitzgerald really live? Who did he hang out with or have a laugh with over a drink? More than ever, the victim himself matters in this case."

"We'll get there."

"Will we?" Juliet questioned. "Do you not find it strange that we know so little about the victim, one so famous? I'm not even talking about the investigation anymore; I'm talking about the John Fitzgerald of yesterday. To have a superhero mopping up after us and not even know his girlfriend's name, his favourite television show."

"Trust the process," Tom insisted. "What case gets solved in a few hours? I don't want you thinking this is all on you to fix."

"Let's go back in," Juliet snapped.

"I'll grab a coffee," Tom insisted. "It's been a long day, bound to get longer."

Juliet allowed Tom to leave her without acknowledgement. Sure, for now there was patience and process. But when the days ticked by in high-profile cases, when the police needed to play politics and wrestle public perception, where would they turn? The same place they'd turned before. *Well, if the mind-reader can't find anything either…*

Back upstairs and Juliet could finally watch John Fitzgerald's father before her. A voluntary interview, she scrutinised and eyeballed Mike behind a one-way mirror all the same.

The FLO Charlotte had been a glorified waitress, pandering to his every demand. In his thoughts Mike leered over

Charlotte as she provided water, food and even a cushion to cater to him. News travelled of the father weeping as he'd identified his son on the table, and the sympathetic instruction was to be as accommodating as possible. Yet time ticked on and comfort provided no answers.

The fuss and attention was clearly something Mike wasn't used to, and he wanted to appreciate it. John Fitzgerald's father was the star of his own show, and Tom had informed her that a meeting with the Queen and Prime Minister awaited him later on. Somewhere else, people were dashing to find a hairdresser, a suit in his size and shoes for his feet so he was presentable for the cameras. Politics, spin, and appearance. The reason they were all together in the first place seemed to be lost in the noise.

Far from the body, the officers had picked a quieter spot for the sit-down with Mike.

Ethan came into the room. "You got anything interesting?"

"He knows nothing," Juliet confirmed. "He's embarrassed by the estrangement and hasn't been letting any of the people he's been speaking to know it. Caught him retelling a childhood story to Charlotte earlier. Never happened."

Ethan let out a cynical laugh as he rubbed his eyes. "Tom was telling me the pub's a dead end."

"Your killer wasn't in that pub. The wine bottle came from elsewhere."

"Trust my luck for a red ball like this case to land on my desk."

"What's the plan with the dad?" Juliet quizzed as she watched Mike stew.

"Charlotte's keeping him occupied and happy, she's been asking him some questions already."

"You want me to speak with him?"

"No need," Ethan acknowledged. "He's not here as a suspect. Stay in here and pick up anything you can, but I'd leave it to Charlotte to be the contact."

Legal advice kept Juliet to minimal contact and involvement with the accused in most cases. Any court would deem her opinion and account inadmissible. Equally, Juliet knew she was to learn nothing of importance from Mike. Watching through the glass, it was the context that appealed to her. In the time before superheroes became a reality, their existence had filled popular culture. Comics, blockbuster films and television serials had a rich history dating back decades. Each universe had their own traits, clichés and rules.

But the life of John Fitzgerald wasn't like fiction.

Unlike the cliché characters in comics, John was no orphan. His father sat in the other room, a rough figure with no special abilities to speak of. A brother and a mother had passed away over the years, and there was no mask or cape to hide behind. Nor was he a billionaire, from another planet or hiding behind a secret identity. No, this was the murder investigation of a working-class boy from the North East who had become a person of spectacular importance for reasons yet unknown.

What interested Juliet most about John's father was the access to the buried history. Had John been a rebellious toddler, shy child or awkward teen – there lay decades of memories backstage and Juliet wanted to shine the light on it.

Equally, another thought was sinking into her consciousness. Mike knowing no answers didn't mean he couldn't get some. *Push the right buttons and the father can learn more about his son in one morning than we can in a week.* An entire morning and early part of the afternoon had passed without a single lead materialising.

Ethan's phone vibrated in his hand, and he stepped out the room to answer it. Like a revolving door, Tom returned with two coffees. "Two sugars, enough milk to make me sick," he said as he handed the coffee over. The same joke, going back years. A lot had changed from the first time they had met; a lot hadn't. After being hired, Juliet had laughed at the trainer before her as he rattled through a checklist regarding the responsibilities of her new role. That man had turned out not to be a trainer, but a partner. And his affection for her, even in the face of Juliet's extraordinary ability, never dampened.

"I feel a bit like a spare part," Juliet said as she warmed her hands on the cup's surface.

"There will be eulogy later," Tom confirmed. "A people-led movement that the politicians have jumped upon. Ethan's asked us to attend."

"Can he not ask me himself? I was just in the room with him. Sometimes I feel like a giant baby," Juliet scoffed.

"Try being the babysitter," Tom countered. "Once upon a time, I used to be a detective."

As Juliet sipped her coffee, from the corner of her eye she watched Charlotte leave the next room, leaving Mike alone. *Push the right buttons and the father can learn more about his son in one morning than we can in a week*. A risky manoeuvre was materialising in her mind, one that was immoral and risked her entire presence in the investigation. If Juliet had access to what was simmering beneath the surface, this could be the one chance they had.

"You forgot the sugars," Juliet stated as she handed Tom back the cup.

"I definitely put sugars in," Tom insisted.

"I'm telling you," Juliet demanded, raising her eyebrows and pointing her finger to her coffee. "You did not."

Doubt stirred in Tom's mind, and Juliet leapt on it. "I can read your mind, you know? I know you're unsure."

Sighing, Tom put his coffee down on the side. "You really rinse the coffee situation when it's my turn."

"Thanks!" Juliet called as Tom left the room. The second he was a moment away, she dashed out of the room. There would be one opportunity for the world's only mind-reader to get access to the victim's father, wade through the depths and layers of such an intimate relationship, regardless of any recent distance. In good conscience she couldn't afford to let the opportunity to pass on ceremony, fluffing up the old man with niceties and chit-chat. Was that what she was here for?

As Juliet entered the room her eyes fell on John's father who looked battered, broken and exhausted. His hair stood up all over the place, thick bags sat under his eyes while his pale skin looked fatigued. A thick, unkempt stubble coated his face, and the image presented before her was of an individual who stopped caring about life a long time ago. The faint smell of sick and alcohol clung to the man's body. The image before Juliet repulsed her.

A heroin-using superhero lay murdered in a nearby room. Juliet *should* play by the rules, but in her head she'd already decided on what her next steps would be. The rulebook had been torn up.

Mike looked up as the door opened. A young woman in her early thirties was entering. Charlotte hadn't mentioned speaking to anyone else, and he felt the hostility in the approaching gaze. When Mike imagined government and police, he did not imagine so many women on the front lines. Hard, aggressive men in uniforms with batons flashed in his mind. The police force and law enforcement had evolved a little since the seventies and eighties.

"I'm not the police," the lady declared as she took a seat. "And I can read every thought that rattles through your brain."

Surely she was messing with him? A journalist who'd broken through the ranks. There were meant to be less than a hundred people like John in the world. Tensing in his seat, Mike regretted his most recent thought process but quickly concluded that the lady was bluffing.

"I've been watching you through the glass," she said, nodding to the mirror. "My name is Juliet Reynolds and I have questions I need your help with. You are one of our best chances of getting up to speed on who your son was and who may have murdered him."

"And why didn't Charlotte mention any interview?" Mike replied. "She's my contact."

"They sent me in to cut through the bullshit."

"You're not meant to be here," Mike concluded, a wry smile forming on his face. "I'm not saying a word until Charlotte is back."

"You don't have to," Juliet said, tapping her head. Leaning back in her chair, her eyes were unflinching as they watched Mike. Confident in her manner, her body language made Mike uneasy. Could she be telling the truth?

"Why did you stop speaking? What happened all those years ago?"

"None of your business," Mike snapped.

"A man hears his son is murdered," Juliet pressed. "It seems strange for him not to do all he could to help with the investigation."

Mike glanced at the glass. How many people were on the other side? Was Charlotte? Suddenly he felt very isolated, shoulders tense, and his trembling hands under the table wouldn't stop.

"It's something I don't like to talk about, that's all," Mike responded as he tried to move the conversation elsewhere.

"Were you involved in the murder of your son?"

The picture of John, cut open on the mortuary table, flashed back in Mike's mind. The face, older than he remembered, soulless. Years of history Mike would never know. "I wasn't," Mike snarled. "I was in Northumberland, for fuck's sake, and we hadn't spoken in years."

"Then what do you have to lose filling me in about what happened all those years ago?"

"I don't like your tone," Mike stated. "And to be blunt, I don't like you."

The atmosphere was delicately balanced. Like a child walking into the room following a heated argument, there was an indescribable weight, beyond something physical.

"Fair enough, I maybe have been a little hostile," Juliet admitted. "But my bosses have instructed me to come interview you, and I know it's a waste of time. You didn't even know your son."

"What the fuck do you know about the relationship with my son?" But Mike got it. John Fitzgerald wasn't just his son. John's murder, not just his business. But the face opposite him was one of only cold, hard expression. There was no heart or sympathy in her eyes.

"What happened?" came the rapid response. "Why did you and John stop talking?"

A curled lip, eyes filled with hatred, Mike spat, his words coated in venom. "You want me to answer your fucking question? I can't. That's your answer. Not that I won't answer, because I can't. I was drunk, so drunk that I couldn't stand, and I said something, can't even remember what. The next morning he'd gone, and he never came back."

Across the table from Juliet, a pair of vicious eyes stared back. The stench of booze was thick in the air. Before her sat a man who had lost all the close family he had. Alone to raise the boy. The information she had on the family life was bare, the next question she wanted to ask was obvious, likely to unsettle Mike.

"Did your problems with alcohol come before or after John ran away from home?"

"Always," Mike answered. He'd calmed a little in his responses but remained agitated by the situation. "Why are you asking about me?"

"I just wanted a sense of the environment John grew up in," was Juliet's measured response. "Not sure why I'm bothering mind, you barely knew him. You hadn't spoken in years."

The statement caused Mike to consider walking out. His anger boiled beneath the surface as he pictured slamming Juliet's head against the table. Mike didn't need to stand for this; his son was dead and he was being treated like he was dirt by a stranger opposite.

"I knew my son," Mike spat. "For sixteen years I put food on his table and clothes on his back. Every meal he ever had, every shirt and every sock came because of *my* graft and *my* discipline. We may not have been close, but don't you dare question my parenting. I was a single father with two young boys. I did the best I could."

"A single father with two young boys so drunk he could barely stand," Juliet recited. "When he left at seventeen, I have it on record that he joined the military before being revealed to the world in the Cherwell fire. Do you know where he went, where he lived, and who he was close to in that period?"

Embarrassment filled up Mike, but Juliet knew she had to verbalise what she was hearing in his thoughts. She didn't have long until someone returned and pulled her out. The answers the case needed weren't there in the room, nor through any amount of questioning would they be. Rage, regret, and resentment. Those were the emotions Juliet needed to tap into. A roll of the dice that might lead to the truth.

"You never called the police or told anybody close to you what had happened, did you?" Juliet said scornfully, her eyes flicking to the glass. "Shame meant that you never looked for him, never attempted to reach out, and so you spent the intermittent years wallowing in self-pity. Earlier on, I had full access to your son's autopsy. Let me tell you what it told us. His body contained heroin in surprisingly large quantities. There was a tattoo on his chest I know you know damn well nothing about, and scarring on his body too. I'm not meant to be in here, let alone tell you that, but I am. Here I am as the world's sole mind-reader and I'm looking for any scrap of information that might tell us how his powers developed, how they were switched off, who he was close to and who may have murdered him. Instead, I'm given a man who can't even look at me straight, he's so drunk. Is there anything you can give me?"

The only way Mike could describe alcohol addiction was

like living with a daily tormentor. It was a bully that knew every one of his delicate, precious hopes, guilty secrets and weaknesses. Daily, it pulled and pinched his invisible puppet strings to manipulate and torture him. The woman Mike was facing was a human embodiment of the nasty bully he craved to bury.

Juliet was right, of course. Outside of raising John in an unstable environment before finally driving him away, Mike had little to offer the investigation in terms of history. John never had an ability, showed no sign of being special when they were together. Anything between then and saving the children at Cherwell School was as big a mystery to Mike as it was to Juliet. The military? No idea. Where he lived? Mike wasn't exactly first on any invite list. Any friends or partners? John would hardly have introduced them to Mike.

Before Mike could answer the final, punching question, the door swung open and another man, stocky and with a face full of rage, burst in. Juliet didn't even resist as the arm grabbed her and ushered out the door. The only company Mike was left with was Juliet's last revelation. Heroin. Like a dagger through the heart, Mike learnt like father, like son, John has been an addict.

For years the silver lining to all that had happened, all that Mike had messed up, was that the boy had turned out okay. Healthy, self-assured and with an incredible arsenal of super-abilities? The man that appeared on the news was more than Mike could have prayed for his son to become. But heroin? Mike had dabbled in several society's vices to numb it all. Alcohol was the cheap poison of choice, but he knew one thing – there was no taking heroin casually.

What had John got himself into?

The fury began as soon as Tom and Juliet hit the quiet of the next room.

"What the fuck was that? They will go ape shit when word gets back to them on this. That man just lost his son and you call him wallowing in self-pity? That same man meets the fucking Queen later on. The press will crucify you."

BLAH, BLAH, BLAH.

Tom may have seemed hard, but was really a mild-mannered individual with a vast amount of patience. An employee with a reputation for doing things by the book, listening to rules and never overstepping the line, it was the exact reason they had paired him with Juliet. The explosion she was witnessing was the consequence of pushing his boundaries to breaking point. But she wasn't sorry. What she'd done was necessary.

"An ability to read people's minds, yet you seem clueless what it's like to be a human being," Tom said coldly.

"Mike Fitzgerald has spent the past few years in a self-destructive spiral with the outcome only ending one way. He barely knew his son, who just died," Juliet detailed calmly as Tom paced, seething. "If I were to be soft on him, pander to him like everyone else, he goes home to mourn and we gain nothing. By going hard on him like that, ripping the delusion right out of his head, he might just go home and question himself a little now. His son was a drug addict. That would shock even the worst father."

"It's always the fathers with you, isn't it," Tom taunted. "Go see a fucking therapist."

Juliet let the insult pass, remained cool. "The shock and knowledge I just gave him will eat him up inside and may get us something useful."

"Or maybe you just signed the death note of a man who has

nobody left," Tom responded. "A dead wife and two dead sons. I don't care if he was a good or an awful father, what he isn't is a tool for you to toy with. Don't you think he's suffered enough? He's an alcoholic who's barely getting by."

"And it's one man versus solving the murder of a superhero," Juliet retorted. "I get it, the man has lost a son, and I went in heavy. But out there? John Fitzgerald doesn't just *die* Tom; whatever and whoever they implicate in his murder, the outcome will be massive. I'm taking the steps that will eventually need to be taken. John Fitzgerald does not just die like that without something bigger going on. Unless we get answers, and soon, this could spiral out of control."

"It's Bowman all over again," Tom yelled. "Screw the case for your own warped sense of justice, right?"

"Here we fucking go," Juliet sniped back. "Bring Will Bowman up again all you want, but I made sure that scumbag never made it back onto the streets. Which is more than can be said for you. If we'd followed all the rules, how many other little girls would have died?"

"I lied for YOU."

"You didn't lie for me," Juliet scorned. "You lied for my ability."

Tom slammed the coffee mug down and stormed out the room. In the meantime Charlotte had returned, looking equally furious as she spoke to Mike through the glass. Ethan would be back soon too. Another scolding, most likely. Any response Juliet could give them would be just more fuel to the fire and no help to her cause. As an agent she was rebellious, forthright and bold. But had that ever gone past the line into cruelty? One last look back through the glass and she saw an old man despondent. Years of being inside the minds of others and she felt no closer or further away to understanding their owners. Outside there was a world trying to glue itself together, while being pulled apart in equal measure.

Where was the sense of urgency?

Chapter Eight

For decades Mike had failed to describe the problem to people like Juliet. How could he when it made little sense to himself? It sounded so simple in his head. Stop. Just stop it. Put the drink down. Tidy the house, clean his shit up and get a job like the rest. When Mike put his head to the problem, the answers were so clear cut. The doctors and lost friends each went through their own journey from optimism to the pits of accepting the cold, hard reality. Most people drank for positive reasons, like social occasions, to celebrate and to let loose at the end of the week. Men like Mike drank for the darkness, not to feel okay but, for a moment, to not feel so bad.

The hour after the interview triggered such levels of second-hand embarrassment, it even shamed Mike's guide for the day, Charlotte, to silence. Mike didn't know if this was better or worse, half-hearted attempts at trying to make the situation better or being left alone to stew in his own public humiliation. All the while there was the image in his head: his son dead on a slab, far from home and where he had begun. There was anger stirring deep, fury at the scorn levelled on him by a complete stranger. Yet Mike reserved most of the anger for himself. Within Juliet's unkind words, little in them proved untrue.

One look in the mirror told Mike all he needed to know. A self-destructing failure of a man. How could a person's gaze not be drawn to all of his faults? Tangled hair in need of both a wash and trim, an unkempt beard sheltering worn, rough skin and tired eyes. Out of view there was regular pus in his socks, nails that bled, not to mention his memory loss. It wasn't just his clothes that smelled; Mike's entire body stank of booze so deep that even scrubbing his skin raw couldn't shed it. Any person who bothered to rest their eyes on such a sorry sight would draw the same conclusions.

Under Ethan's orders, accompanied by Charlotte, they whisked Mike away from the police station. That evening there were plans at the palace. Royalty, the Prime Minister and a vast array of other members of high society. Delicately, Charlotte pitched a haircut, suit fitting and an assortment of other things to occupy the time. Only if Mike wished, of course. But what else was he going to do?

All afternoon there were commiserations, handshakes and pitying eyes. A barber tamed Mike's ragged mane, tried to chit chat, liven up the situation with small talk. Eventually the trim and wash was completed in silence. The tailor, the epitome of professionalism, fared better. With his measuring tape and needles, he made rapid work of measuring Mike for a suit, with barely a word uttered.

As Mike admired himself in the mirror, the self-destructing man had momentarily disappeared; the face one he no longer recognised. Is this what another life could have been like? The longer he stared, the more the sense of failure within himself stirred.

"I need a smoke," Mike stated rather than requested. Tears had welled up in his eyes as he handed back the suit jacket.

Charlotte did nothing to stop him.

Lost in a labyrinth of corridors and meeting rooms, Mike found the first fire exit he could and walked down the metal stairs. An alarm sounded, but there would be a lot more going on around the place than one fire alarm.

Downstairs, at least there was a bench, out of sight of any road or entrance. Caged and with big black bars around its perimeter, Mike laughed at how the life of a smoker had deteriorated over the course of his lifetime. Once seen as glamorous, an edgy habit of rock-gods and movie-stars, the health warnings had kicked in and left it to ordinary people in pubs, clubs and offices. Then the smoking ban had come in, which forced men like Mike out of their nice warm environment and out into the bitter cold. Caged like misbehaving toddlers, you could often find smokers round the corner in a cloud of smoke, usually with a fence to keep them in place. The bench with only a tree for company proved the extent of the natural views in London. Northumberland had spoilt him.

As Mike took a spot on the empty bench, a weight of rage left upon the first inhale. *Didn't know his own son?* Mike remembered his boy all right. Both of them. Mike recalled the first time John had opted to run away and packed a bag as he headed for the door. A small cartoon backpack filled with underpants and a teddy bear. The fury in his face as Mike could only laugh rather than stop the four-year-old making his momentous statement. Mike also remembered the school play where John had got bored midway through and crawled off stage to join his mother and father, despite it being his turn. As fellow parents laughed, a junior teacher desperately tried to coax the child back to the stage but John was having none of it.

He thought of David too, how different the boys had been. The first sports day of the first-born child had been magnificent. Egg and spoon race, coconut toss, the sack race: whatever the sport, David mopped up the medals. Years later John would often get upset as he finished last, but David had never had such problems. As if he was born for sport, they said. Mike remembered basking in the other parents' praise of David.

Mike had been a poor father – in a shock to nobody the flawed person had grown into a flawed parent. But not be there for his own kids? That was a goddamn lie. Reminiscing about those past days, Mike barely noticed the approaching figure.

"Do you need a light?" came a foreign voice and jolted Mike from his thinking. Stood above him was a small man with hard eyes. He pointed at Mike's unlit second cigarette, still fumbling in his hands. He couldn't even remember the first.

Mike nodded, and the man flicked his fingers into a flame. Outstretching it, he lit the end and lit his own.

"Spanish?" Mike said, not wanting to focus on the obvious super-ability.

"Italiano," came the proud response, and the man took a seat. "Wish I was there. England and her crazy cigarette prices."

"In London, nearly twenty pounds," Mike said incredulously as he shook the packet.

"We'd have revolted by now," the Italian said with a shake of his head, taking a drag.

Mike agreed as he puffed on his own. "Robbing bastards."

The man laughed and a brief pause occurred as they enjoyed a token inhale of their expensive luxury.

"My name is Marco," the Italian said as he outstretched a hand. "Are you Fitzgerald's father?"

Fifty seconds, no more, and Mike was back on his son. He nodded. "Did you know him?"

"I did," said the man, to Mike's surprise. And then after a brief pause Marco continued. "A bit of a prick, but I'm as sorry and shocked as everyone else."

Mike laughed at Marco's honesty. He took a moment to look a little closer at the figure next to him. To match his brutal eyes, there was a strong jawline, a nose that looked like it had taken a few hits. The Italian was young, in good shape, although small in stature.

"How did you know him?"

"Work," Marco began. "Back in the old days, before it was all public. The UK government had quite a collection of us. Now it's just Juliet. I'm here as a favour from the Italian government, just got rushed over in case I'm needed. Mostly there's been handshakes and photographs so far."

"I met Juliet," Mike replied. "She was charming."

Marco smiled. "Juliet has her own way of working. Your boy had his and I have mine."

"Did he ever talk about the past?"

"Not that kind of relationship," Marco began. "We talked about books. Your boy, he was a serious person and liked his serious reading. Me? I'm a fiction kind of guy – give me a generic police book with a leading detective estranged from his daughter and a serial killer to catch. Fitzgerald? He was all about the philosophy, the deeper meaning and all that stuff. I'll admit I'm thin on that front."

"You're not the only one," Mike chipped in.

"Well, we couldn't really talk about books in the traditional sense, having such opposite tastes. We could talk about what made a good character, though, how best to tell a story. I'm talking a handful of conversations over several years here, but enough for a pattern to emerge. John was the person constantly chasing the *why*. He wanted to know the motivations, the drive and the impact of characters and decisions. There was a lot of non-fiction, autobiographies of Holocaust survivors, Malcolm X or former politicians. I always thought that was funny. In future decades, he'd be reading memoirs of people he had met and lived through. I guess... well... your boy liked to learn a little something about the world."

"And you?"

"Ha! While your boy was the person chasing the why, I'm the reader who didn't need care about it. The thrill of the adventure, the chase, and the journey is what I liked. A detective catching the serial killer? It wasn't about the killer, the reasons they both did it. No, for me it was the fight along the way I responded to. Call me uncultured but give me a blockbuster film over an artsy one any day. How about you?"

"I can't read for shit," Mike replied candidly.

"Not a fan?"

"I can't read at all."

Marco replied wide-eyed in surprise. "I would not have guessed such a man to be your boy."

Mike forced a smile. A recurring theme.

"Did he ever mention me?" Mike asked, sucking up the detectable shame.

"Once," the Italian answered.

Mike looked at the man next to him. His hard eyes weren't joking, and sarcasm was not something that seemed compatible with him. A straight talker, Mike knew he'd hear no white lies or false truths.

"We had been doing a mission in Africa someplace, one shithole or another. Some dictator had overstepped his mark, so they sent in the agents with physical abilities to sort it out. Years before, any of it went public or anything... and afterwards we needed a cigarette. Many of the people we were fighting were victims themselves, creations of their place of birth. Fucks with you, you know? Anyway, we were talking about upbringing, fathers, and eventually you came up."

Mike's shoulder's tensed, but he remained calm in the face of another person's views on his parenting. After one scolding this afternoon, how bad could a second one be?

"John told me a story once, from early in his childhood. A Friday night, he was due to be taken to a birthday party. An enormous deal, John told me, as he never got invited anywhere. Mum working, he was in the house waiting for you to bring his brother home from football practice. The minutes ticked by. He was late, becoming later and later, and finally you came in with your other son. Bag of chips in hand, you'd taken him for a takeaway after. John said nothing and went to his room."

The words did little to stir emotion in Mike. What struck him was that he had no memory of the moment at all.

"I asked John why he told me that story," Marco admitted. "Why that one in particular? All he said was, 'that was the man he was.' The next time we spoke, he seemed embarrassed about bringing it up. We went no further."

"I was there," Mike snapped back rapidly. "For seventeen years I was there."

"He never said you weren't."

"I was there," Mike repeated, but Marco seemed uninterested.

The Italian puffed again on his cigarette. "I have a baby girl now, she's three. Already she talks back, even though she barely knows a handful of words. I would not change her developing little personality for the world. Parenting changes you, terrifies you. Here you have this little bundle of nothing, and you're trying to teach them all that you know and correct all the mistakes you have made. But every child is a legacy of their nature and their nurture. She will cry, I will hurt her and she will hurt me. Parenting is imperfect; I will do the best I can and the rest I cannot control. You cannot change the man you were. He turned out okay and did more good than most could ever dream of. A piece of that is yours."

Mike remained silent, the words soothing. For maybe half a minute the pair finished their cigarettes in silence before Marco got to his feet and stamped his out.

"I'm sorry about your boy."

"Me too," Mike nodded.

Thick and fast, two memories bounced in Mike's head. The young boy attempting to run away from home and the one Marco had created, a boy waiting for a birthday party. The same life, the same two people involved, yet dramatically different outcomes. The third, the body, joined soon enough.

Juliet had suggested he was wallowing in self-pity. Mike considered for a few moments whether he agreed. Self-pity implied vanity, self-centredness. A person like that, thought Mike, drank out of weakness and lack of willpower. Mike would be the first to join in the criticism, the blame for every mistake, the destruction and consequence of everything falling back on him and the drink.

It was not weakness that made Mike drink. No – it was the

addiction that made Mike weak, and until he found a way of no longer needing the medicine, he would remain that way. Long ago he had half-expected a defining moment, a rock bottom to build back up from. Maggie had passed away of cancer and left him to raise two young boys. David had passed away and so the medicine only came in larger quantities. By the time John left, any hope of a decisive moment had long since faded.

Since then, Mike had been waiting. Waiting to die? He could no longer say.

Chapter Nine

The morning passed into early afternoon with Juliet in the same waiting room. A television screen reporting round-the-clock coverage of the John Fitzgerald murder struggled to fill the airtime with no developments.

World leaders had provided speeches, members of parliament had been interviewed for reactions. Gradually, every person of any standing in society offered their take. Juliet had taken it upon herself to switch the television off when a reaction interview with a television celebrity chef began. The ticking clock next to the screen proved more scintillating.

Streams of people came and went. Friendly faces flicked in Juliet's direction, others grave and bitter. They always wore their thoughts on their sleeve, only a little digging in their brains necessary. They had looked over any informants and come up empty, hoping that a fellow officer had better luck.

Charlotte and Mike had left the police station not long after the interview, the Queen and Prime Minister waiting to offer their private condolences. Ethan's communication now came only via Tom, his initial enthusiasm replaced by distance. As the senior officer, if he didn't want Juliet's help there was nobody who could really make him use it. The red ball case resembled a stick of dynamite, and he now deemed Juliet a risk, seeing it blowing up in his face.

When Tom came back, his anger had subsided, replaced with a coldness. "The impromptu candle eulogy is gaining momentum. A mass gathering of sorts outside of Buckingham Palace. Already it's gaining traction on social media with MPs, celebrities and anyone with any societal weight expected to be present. Ethan wants you inside their heads. Anything radical or out of the ordinary recorded for interviews. Somebody there might know who did it," Tom commanded.

"Why Buckingham Palace?" Juliet quizzed.

"Where else do the British go in times of need?" Tom answered, still with stern eyes. "Truth is, they're tweaking Operation London Bridge which had been designed for the death of the Queen. They have trained the police and military to have such an occasion held there."

"Is there a plan before then?"

"Home," Tom stated with a furious expression on his face. Holding back the emotion no longer, he said, "He was in pieces after you left."

Admittedly Juliet felt guilt towards the father she had berated earlier. The man wasn't a criminal, but equally he had more potential than any of them to discover the key to the murder. Break a few eggs to make an omelette.

"We'll pick you up at seven," Tom called from the car. "If anybody of interest appears, I'll be back before then. Keep your phone on."

Back at her flat after being dropped off, Juliet mulled over what to do until she was next needed. If a witness or person of interest were to appear, they would immediately call her back into action, but until that happened there was little she could offer above the sea of other officers out in the field seeking information.

Mid-afternoon and there was no need to rest; her body regimented to early starts and early finishes. It would be a while before the necessity of sleep reared its head.

To make up for her interrupted run, a half-hour workout appealed. Exercise outside sounded pleasant, the air warm and any bitterness in the air months away. Yet as Juliet pictured doing it, with all the people and all that was going on, being outside would only remind her further of John.

Changing into some gym gear, rolling out an exercise mat and flicking on a playlist, Juliet stretched. The perfect antidote to a day that made little sense.

A high-intensity workout followed, with testing planks and a disgusting amount of burpees thrown in – core exercises designed to burn and stretch Juliet to her physical limit. In only half an hour, her tension and stress relieved, her physical and mental energy was boosted, and her sense of well-being restored. Anything that got her moving helped, but Juliet got a bigger benefit by paying attention instead of zoning out.

When Juliet exercised, it went deeper than that. She noticed the sensation of her feet hitting the ground, the rhythm of her breathing, the feeling of the wind on her skin. By adding this mindfulness element, really focusing on her body and how it felt when she exercised, she not only improved her physical condition, but could interrupt the flow of constant worries running through her head.

Once done Juliet opted for a shower, her music loud and pumping as she let the water run. She had a two-bedroom flat all to herself in the centre of London. At twenty-eight, single and with no qualifications past school, there were few occupations of a self-made nature that would let her live in a place like she did. House prices being the way they were, and the gap between wages and property only increasing, Juliet took a moment to cast a fresh eye over her flat. Since it came as part of the deal of her employment she paid no rent, and was given allowances for food, clothes and travel all on top of her hefty wage. Juliet need only ask and a bigger television, all-inclusive holiday, or the latest piece of tech would materialise. The British government would pay a heavy fee to keep her services rather than see the world's only known mind-reader move sides.

Stepping into the shower, she let the water run over her shoulders. 'Married to the job' was a phrase thrown around often, but that wasn't really the truth. Divorced from everything else was a closer description, and Juliet wasn't talking about the last hour. In school, friendships and hobbies had seemed so easy. There was an abundance of after-school activities, free time and hundreds of people thrown together. The day it ended, there was a void. She had been lucky enough to walk into employment right away – not only that, a high-flying lifestyle and a career for life. Yet after nearly a decade, Juliet had become agitated.

Being able to read minds was an exotic ability. Every thought, feeling or opinion visible to just one person was an inquisitive person's fantasy. Reality versus expectation was another thing. Imagine every insecurity being confirmed, whether it's a person's intention or not. That time a joke fell flat, you thought you looked bloated in a dress or were embarrassed in a situation, with the running commentary of every witness entering your own mind one word at a time. Yet on the flip side, every suspicion became validated. Is that cute guy at the bar checking me out? Words like *attractive* and *fit* emerge from his mind. Over the years Juliet had grown used to the wildness and untamed nature of the human mind. From emotions of the deepest love to passionate hatred in the matter of one conversation, the individual sat with a physical poker face the entire time. Once it had baffled her, but now it was just part of her life.

The glow of human thoughts, like everything, faded. As Juliet lathered foam over her body, she tried to calculate how many times she had undertaken the same menial tasks of brushing her teeth, trimming her nails and washing her hair. Juliet could say the same for her ability. Once the human brain had been wonderously complex, the secrets and thoughts exciting and devilish. But over time patterns emerged, and the dull reality of day-to-day life was stark. Television shows, news stories, workplace drama and home life arguments were ninety percent of what ran through a person's mind. Without context, it was even more irrelevant to Juliet than it was to the original owner.

Eventually work became all that was exciting. Cases at least – murders, missing person cases and the rest – offered a rare, thrilling insight into darker emotions, motives and thoughts not associated with the tedious day-to-day lives of others. In a world that was tiring Juliet, the cases broke the monotony. Over time, she lost herself in the work, the investigations and the interviews. Once an escape from reality, the shadows had eventually become her new home and left her distant from the world left behind.

Stepping away from the water, Juliet rubbed conditioner in and watched the water fall as she waited. Thoughts of another average person entered her brain, Mike Fitzgerald. Juliet's shoulders sank as the memory flooded back. A man with nobody left, an existence empty since the finality of youth, career and family life all ended. On the day the world stood still to mourn his son, a point of pride, Juliet had proved a shattering intrusion.

An image entirely constructed in her own mind manifested itself. Mike, weeks down the line, alone in a dreary, cold and empty house, exhaling with a bottle of rum emptied before him. The media fanfare and adulation dead. The monotony of day-to-day living was all that remained. A belt round his neck, Mike wondering how long it would take for someone to notice.

Sickened, Juliet interrupted her thoughts as she slid back under the warm water. Despite the steamy air and warmed skin, she suddenly felt a shiver run through her. The human brain was complex and fragile; it needed less pressure than one imagined in cracking the contents. Through her own actions, what had she stirred within John's father?

Rinsing the last of the soap from her body and hair, Juliet's thoughts momentarily drifted to her own father. Juliet switched the water off the second that happened, and grabbed a towel. There was enough father-and-child relationship issues in her head for one day.

A car came round to pick Juliet up at around seven. The police had toiled, but nothing concrete answered any of the questions surrounding the investigation. The running theory was that John flew down, and the incident took place. With the slim number of individuals in the area, photos of the grainy CCTV images were being circulated while cell towers and GPS signals of mobile phones in the area were traced to find owners.

Tests on those with abilities were yielding little in discovering how John Fitzgerald's ability had shut down. Tests on the impact of opioids and heroin revealed nothing between ability and functionality, while nobody questioned had any history of their powers being able to shut themselves off.

Tom's attitude had cooled in the hours since he and Juliet had last seen each other. From briefing to briefing they had dragged him along, learning little new or helpful information. Twelve hours after the murder and with no breakthrough in sight anywhere, nervousness was seeping through the investigation. They weren't at the stage for desperate measures just yet, but once the public's shock settled down, there was fear of what could come next.

Describing the life of one of the mega cities of the world like New York and London was difficult. The major global cities operated to a clock and calendar they created themselves. Go time, all the time. No matter what time the clock showed, what weather stood overhead in the sky or the colour of the trees, the city never halted. Sure, there were differences. The corporate bustle of the day made way for the loveable grimness of the night scene, but wedged in the gap was a city always awake.

The evening of John's candle eulogy, the streets were basking in light. Summer, warm under the cloudless sky and heat, contrasted to the mood of the people. In ordinary times, barbeques and sunbathing would be the main event. In cities the world over, the public had put pleasantries on hold to show their respect. There were to be speakers, Chinese lanterns and candles in places for when it was dark enough. They planned a minute's silence.

There was something uniquely British about having it centred around the home of the royal household. As it had hosted the end of the war in Europe with victory, the palace was to act as a unifying location in greyer times. The Queen's grandson was to make a speech, as was the Prime Minister, with hundreds of politicians, major figures and celebrities in attendance. The funeral would come later – a proper burial and celebration of John's life. But for now, the public needed something to give sense to the day.

Escorts took Juliet to the front shortly before The Mall was closed off and already-huge numbers of people were out in force for the historic event. Weaving past the crowds like a sniper, Juliet could pick out flashes and glimpses in the mood of random people. A sense of uncertainty stared the population in the face, and a secure future only a day ago was now absent. Mothers held their children's hands a fraction tighter. Police officers and soldiers' eyes had become a little warier. Yet in numbers they came, united in grief and a fragile harmony.

They fortified The Mall with a heavy police and military presence and as Juliet waited, she listened out for what stories filtered through. Accounts were emerging of Britons forced to close shops and the sporting events cancelled, lest they feel the rage of tear-stained hordes. Mass hysteria felt like it was brewing, the stiff upper lip replaced by a whipped-up sentimentality. What Juliet saw in the crowds was not the characteristic coolness and grit of the population, but a baying mob with candles, teddy bears and poems.

Yet the situation forced Juliet's attention to other people or proceedings. There was a job to do. Gigantic screens prepared at impressively short notice focused in on the crowds of people. Montages and footage of the Cherwell School rescue; crowd control in Detroit and Sudan. Buoyant cheers erupted at the footage of rescues and sights of food being given out on the streets of Afghanistan. British flags, posters of John Fitzgerald, and tearful faces filled a crowd there to appreciate an icon.

"Every politician in the country is present here today," Tom whispered as he lent in close to her arm. "Not only that, but security officials, undercover agents, and anyone of remote standing in British society. Keep alert and keep your ability agile. We will not get another opportunity like this to get this many people free and in the open like this."

Tom let go of Juliet's arm, allowing her to wander. Up and down The Mall, there were thousands of people. Fear, anger, frustration and sadness swept over them in waves, switching from one emotion to the next in round after round. The herd mentality was a thick reality, as the people within it absorbed like sponges and squeezed out their own emotions just as easily between themselves.

On a small makeshift stage, one of the country's brightest musical talents acoustically played several ballads. As the crowds swayed and mourned, Juliet picked person after person out of the VIP enclosure. Their thoughts were largely the same: devastation and worry for the future. There was no suspicion, joy or anything out of place amongst them. The flash of paparazzi and rolling of television cameras was the typical signal that someone important had arrived, and at this point Juliet would chime in.

A cabinet minister, a handful of MPs and television personalities came and went with nothing more than superficial encounters on their minds. They'd met John at dinners, award ceremonies, and recalled fondly the same heroic images and stories as everyone else. Nothing special, nothing beneath a surface-level encounter. For over an hour they waited as the music played and television cameras rolled. If somebody wanted publicity, or to suggest they had a special relationship with John Fitzgerald, now was the time to do it.

Somewhere between the music, speeches and dedications, the Prime Minister stepped onto the podium and a hush fell across the crowd. His face worn and pale, Juliet got the sense that there had not been a break in his schedule since the minute they had found John's body. Politics had never particularly interested her. Regarding her career, a change-over of Home Secretary or leader had no visible impact on the day-to-day operations she was a part of. Juliet left the passion and emotions surrounding politics to others.

What Juliet could acknowledge was the readiness of the crowd to hang on George Eden's every word. There was no political leaning or opinion in any of the faces or thoughts that Juliet paid attention to. The people needed a leader, a person to haul them through the tough times to come, regardless of political leaning or ideology. With his grey hair, teddy-bear physique and funereal suit, the figure before them was far from a slick presidential figure with a polished smile for television. But all the same the people listened.

"I stand before you today in what could go down in history as the greatest individual loss of our nation. But I want to reassure you all that it does not have to be that way.

"Just over ten years ago, an ordinary citizen with extraordinary abilities, in whose symbolic shadow we stand today, did the right thing. In a world he had no idea would accept him, John Fitzgerald risked everything and intervened. The decision to not walk by is one we celebrate today, eternally grateful that it showed the measure of the man we mourn here, together. The purest of us in need. Children lived to survive another day because of his sacrifice. A joyous daybreak and a beacon of hope in a decade where fear had driven the Western world into war and distrust.

"Ten years later I speak of sacrifice because it is now our turn to be martyrs. I ask all those out there listening today to be our own Samaritans that refuse to take the simple path, refuse to walk on by. It would be easy in the coming weeks, months and years to forget the world John temporarily saved us from. The darkness provides shelter, comfort and tranquillity. Yet it is in the light, where we can do the most good.

"It would be fatal for the world to underestimate the urgency of the moment. The thirst for vengeance and revenge is heavy, and I make no light of the struggle for answers. Out there somewhere is an agent of chaos, a murderer who we will bring to justice. Yet it is key that, to achieve this justice, we do not forsake our dignity and humanity. Fear and hatred is degenerative. John did not stand for it, and the society he leaves behind will become his true legacy.

"We do not walk alone. We are not alone. Together we must make the pledge we remain united."

The crowd rapturously applauded. As the Prime Minister took a moment to scan the crowd, he fixed his glasses and internalised the situation. The speech had done its job, his words echoing not just into the ink of the newspapers or the screens over the world, but into history too. They, the masses, sucked it up. *We are civilised.*

Returning to the crowd, Juliet drowned out many of the further speeches and acts on the stage. Swimming around a VIP section near the front were many of the celebrities and the media circus. The majority were too busy or too concerned elsewhere to offer much of use, but escorted by a bodyguard, there was one woman who was the first to break through the normality.

The photographers snapped at her as she removed the big brown sunglasses to reveal eyes reddened from crying and a makeup-free face. She bowed her head and completed her performance by waving away television cameras, looking upset. Juliet knew this was the case as the woman's thought process at the time was coaching herself through it step by step. She'd make the magazines and the montages of mourning. *Slick work*, she thought to herself, *John would have approved.*

The glimpse of the sentence spun Juliet into action. "Who was that lady?" Juliet asked aloud to one photographer.

"Candice Crawford," came the reply. "Model, businesswoman and actress. They used to be an item."

The statement shocked Juliet. From the widespread coverage and intense reading she had ingested in the last few hours, what struck her as odd was the lack of obvious relationships in John's life. On stage was his estranged father with no other immediate family, alongside royalty and elected politicians. There were no friends and no ties to anybody. All the snippets were of his heroics, actions and consequences of his work. Nothing beneath the surface level or talk of what he was like behind closed doors.

The Queen's grandson and the third-in-line for the throne was speaking. The speech itself caught Juliet's eye, but her attention was broken by movement elsewhere.

"The most important title you can carry is that of a citizen. I ask you not to be lawyers, office workers, cleaners or account managers. I ask you to be neighbours, citizens and pillars of your community."

Keeping her attention fixed on the speech, Juliet noticed several officers speaking into radios and rapidly moving back away from the stage. *Bag. Unattended. Bomb.* The ultimate word repeated over and over in the thoughts of the surrounding officers.

"I remind you that history doesn't always follow a straight line. Sometimes we shuffle a few steps back to move forward. We step sideways or we zig-zag, but ultimately we progress. That requires citizens to fight for that future. As this first night without John draws in, it is too soon to ask for this world's brave population to tackle this ugly reality we face – but later, I hope, perspective prevails.

On stage there were several whispers as the Queen and Prime Minister were, as subtly as possible, moved off-stage and flanked by security personnel. Somebody must have given the Prince a signal, for his pace momentarily slowed and his words stiffened. Yet he continued, and the crowd continued to consume his words without alarm or noticing anything out of the ordinary.

"We live day to day with deadlines and the latest ever-refreshing news feed, and it fills us with anxieties and fear. Be reminded that we are a small link in the great chain of human history, and if the last couple of decades have shown us anything, it should be evidence of what can come from unity. We must do the best we can with the time and opportunity allotted to us. We–"

The sound of a single gunshot crackled over the crowd, and in seconds the scene was one of chaos. Security swarmed the figures on stage as thousands panicked. There was a crush as people next to the barriers were pressed up against the metal.

Panic, fear and concern screeched in Juliet's mind. Her eyes darted all around her. Soldiers and police frantically trying to calm the situation and stop a crush. The stage and VIP area had emptied but quickly became flooded with people as the contained broke free.

A shoulder knocked into the back of Juliet, sending her sprawling to the floor. In the shock and confusion, something hit Juliet several more times in what quickly became clear were feet. Again and again, they stamped into her face, arms and body. The light above her became dazzling, fragmented as she tried to haul herself up but ended up kicked back down in the chaos.

Hands clawing at trouser legs, jumpers and bags, Juliet tried to haul herself upright. Kicks to the chest were leaving her breathless, her chest tight. A knock to the head and she was on the floor once more, the pain everywhere and her head spinning. Darkness.

Someone was shaking her, trying to talk to her.

And then everything went black.

Chapter Ten

Since childhood Mike had been a keen Newcastle United fan, if keen could ever be the right word for supporters of his club. Decades without major honours, plus near-misses and relegations, Mike claimed to support Newcastle United but never really felt they supported him back. There was a heartbreak and grit associated with the fabric that stitched the club together. Even a decade with Alan Shearer, one of the greatest strikers to ever play the game, couldn't stop the sorrow year after year. Yet the goals, the passion and the chant of the crowds was enough to always draw him back in.

Supporting the football club was more than that, though. Newcastle was one city. An accent, a passion and a fury that pumped through his veins. There could be no other club or place to call home. Towns and countryside that buffered the city would all proudly call themselves the sacred word: Geordie. Derby days were the most important of the year, when an entire region would lock down and go to war. There was no way to describe such a buzz that vibrated round the people and the places on those days. In their own bubble, outside of tournaments or league positions, the derby had it all. Beat Sunderland at all costs, and that was that.

Sat awkwardly to the side on stage, Mike overlooked a crowd louder and larger than any he had ever seen at St James' Park. Men, women and children of all cultures and ages had poured into every available space just to pay tribute to his son. Was there a million out there? Mike had no way of telling, but as they had driven him through the streets, it seemed like few people in the capital city remained home.

Earlier, the apologies had come thick and fast. Talk of an investigation, punishments and discipline for Juliet and her actions. Mike nodded along, exhausted; he wanted to be back in the North East and far away from all the noise.

That wasn't to be the plan. "You're to meet the Queen and the Prime Minister," Charlotte said as a makeup artist came in. "We need you looking good for the cameras; all the celebrities and people on TV wear it to make them look less shiny."

Pinned to his seat, Mike grimaced as they put powder and unknown creams over his face. If the men from the pits or the working-men's club could see him now, they would have a laughing fit. What made it worse as Mike looked in the mirror, yellow eyes and red nose absent, was that he thought he looked better for it – although that was a secret he vowed to take to the grave.

Whisked off to the palace, Mike had absolutely no idea what they meant for him to do when introduced to the Queen. Charlotte quickly rattled off instructions. "For men you do a neck bow, which is from the head only, whilst I'll do a small curtsy," she said quickly. "On presentation to the Queen, the correct formal address is 'Your Majesty' and subsequently 'Ma'am', pronounced with a short 'a' as in 'jam'. Considering the circumstances don't worry if you appear nervous, people do all the time and it's behind closed doors."

Hands trembling, Mike did exactly what he was told and answered only when spoken to. The Queen had a lot to say – that John was a tremendous loss to not only the people of the country but the wider world – and she was grateful for all of his years of service. Mike had to admit he liked her a lot. Later, Prime Minister George Eden introduced himself and echoed similar words of tribute. Mike couldn't resist revealing he was a trade union man and a lifelong Labour supporter. The Prime Minister hadn't quite known what to say.

Once the small talk and ceremony had occurred at the palace, various faces pushed and led Mike towards a constructed stage on The Mall. Not part of the ceremony, he instead got to watch from a VIP section as the various artists play mournful songs. Mike recognised none of them, music not really being his thing, but the sentiment was nice.

Instead, Mike's attention focused on the buoyant crowd. Thousands of faces held thousands of flags aloft. With it being summer, it would remain light for at least twenty minutes more. A speech from the Prime Minister was to follow and some pop star was to sing the national anthem.

Earlier Mike had necked enough complimentary wine to maintain a suitable level of drunkenness amidst all the noise and bustle happening around him. The cameras kept to the crowds and stage where Mike watched a lovely speech by the Prime Minister and the Queen's grandson. Mike settled, enjoying the video tributes and footage of heroism on the gigantic screens, and the buoyant atmosphere of the crowd. The event was a celebration of life rather than a mourning.

But somewhere in the speeches, the crowd erupted. Drunk Mike could barely pinpoint when the mad scramble started, but one moment he looked up and people were scattering everywhere. Security had already taken care of the Queen and Prime Minister, the stage swarming with people as the barriers crumbled. Hands grabbed for Mike, but he shoved them away and stumbled towards the danger the public were running from.

Who was the enemy and what had started it? Something drew Mike to the gunshots and screams. Occasionally he was almost knocked off his feet as people crashed away from the danger, but soon Mike found shelter behind riot police trying to regain control.

A helicopter spilling light from above in a quiet ego, Mike pictured John crashing from the sky and eliminating the whole mob of the fuckers causing the chaos. On the pickets they had been fighting for something. Who had tarnished such an event? The armed officers held a line as Mike, caught up in the mobs and escaping crowds, could not help but be carried away from the palace. The situation was akin to a scrum as shoulders slammed into Mike from every side. In the darkness, the drunkenness and the scuffles, Mike swore he saw faces below the rushing people.

With streaming eyes, Mike eventually dragged himself out of the thick of the danger and away from the fury. Catching his breath in that moment, the reality of his situation set in. No phone, no wallet and in a capital city a hundred miles from home, Mike did not understand where to go or what to do.

An argument with a seventeen-year-old boy in what felt like another life came to his mind. Drunk, angry and looking for a punching bag, it was often the boy who ended up being knocked about verbally and physically. He'd hit him, hadn't he? The night that John left, Mike remembered with shame he may have hit him. What made it worse was that he couldn't differentiate that night from all the rest. A scrap, some traded blows, Mike would later feel pride in some of those moments watching the way his son responded. John took it; he threw back. Mike had deserved everything, the drunken fool.

Had John felt this way? Alone in a park, stumbling through the darkness towards the unforgiving city lights, Mike couldn't ditch the weight of loneliness hanging around his neck. Only a boy, had he sacrificed his only remaining son to a fate like this? Alone in a world far from home and nobody to lean on?

With every stumbling footstep, Mike loathed the feeling that he was following in John's.

Chapter Eleven

Juliet's head stirred as her vision returned. Flat on her back above the covers on a bed. Somebody had removed her shoes. Curtains drawn. Dark. A person was watching the news with his back to her. A hotel room? Hers? The screen displayed a simple headline: SUSPECT IN CUSTODY. A chair for show, uncomfortable and brought close to the screen. Soldiers, noise, the crush of a crowd. Darkness. The screen read a simple headline; Suspect in custody. Tom in the chair.

When Juliet next awoke her head was clearer, and the darkness had lifted. A wide window to the side had by this point illuminated the room somewhat. Rather than a hotel, she was in a hospital and judging by the faint granite sheen over the outside world, she gathered the day was just about breaking. Five or six in the morning was her best guess.

Agony swept through her body as soon as Juliet dared to lean forward. Her chest tightly bandaged, she guessed she'd broken a rib or two. Letting a hand slide over her body, Juliet found her head similarly wrapped and a cast on her right arm. Left eye swollen, lips dry and cracked, Juliet was a hell of a state. Without a mobile phone or screen in reach, she felt useless and limp where she lay.

In immense pain, Juliet hauled herself to her feet and staggered away from the bed. There was no private room, and in her open ward the other five patients looked fast asleep. Yet as she manoeuvred her way out of the main door, a startled Tom jumped to his feet. In a chair outside, he'd been snoozing.

"What are you doing up?" he half-yelled before stifling his voice. "You should be in bed."

"My legs work just fine," Juliet sneered. "We're going for a coffee."

Knowing the battle probably wasn't worth happening, Tom acquiesced as Juliet dragged herself down the empty corridors. Her estimation of five in the morning proved correct. The odd nurse on night duty wandered the halls, but they had the place to themselves aside from that.

"So what happened?" Juliet said, breaching the subject. "I heard a bomb."

"No bomb," replied Tom as he ambled by her side. "Someone left a bag unattended. A member of the public swore blind they saw wires. Everybody was tense, on alert and in a panic. Emotions running that high. It was foolish to have something so public and so soon. One soldier with a gun misfired his weapon at nobody and in error, and the whole circus exploded. Crushes, trampling as everyone tried to escape what turned out to be a figment of their imagination. Eighty injured ranging from severe to critical conditions, luckily no dead. It was madness."

Eighty injured over nothing. Juliet had no words. Earlier she had wanted to joke about her bandages and cast, but not now. Remembrance of the weight, the rushing feet over her body and the sensation of air being trampled out her lungs remained. Pure isolated luck left her alive.

The pair took residence on some hard, plastic seats. "Coffee, white with two sugars," Juliet joked to a stone-faced Tom. "Enough to make you sick."

"They've got the killer," Tom stated as he choked down a sip of vending machine coffee, still hardened to any attempt at humour. "Pretty much certain at this stage."

"Who was it?" Juliet replied, deflating a little with the news.

"A drug addict, by the name of Casper Smith," Tom answered. "Police arrested him in this hospital a few hours ago. A member of the public reported a dead body. They had found him overdosed in an alleyway soaked in blood. Turned out he was very much alive and when paramedics found no deep wounds on him, they got in touch with the police."

"John Fitzgerald's blood?" Juliet questioned.

Tom nodded before chugging down another mouthful. "Next thing that nabbed him was an image on CCTV of him in the area. This corroborated an eyewitness account placing having him sleeping rough in an empty office building the last week nearby. When nurses first sobered him up enough, he sobbed and drooled enough of an apology for what he did. Guy was so strung out he didn't know his victim was John Fitzgerald."

"You really buy that?" Juliet scorned. "That some strung-out drug addict with a broken bottle could kill John Fitzgerald?"

"It's both anticlimactic and implausible," Tom admitted. "And yet believable at the same time."

When Juliet raised a surprised eyebrow behind the bandages, Tom continued.

"All along the murder scene didn't sit right. Even if it was an inside job or an assassination, the murder was sloppy, brutal, slow and barbaric. If you would kill someone famed for being able to deflect bullets and regenerate, you would not take your time, not chance a broken bottle in some alleyway. There's more to it, no doubt about it, and the murderer we have in our midst is not the same man responsible for John's powers being switched off. But as for the act itself? I think we have him."

"I want to see him," Juliet stated. "I don't care who you have to talk to, I want to get inside that head and see for myself."

"And nobody will stop you," Tom acknowledged. "It was one of the first things I asked, and I've heard nothing but encouragement since."

The answer fell flat in Juliet's stomach. There should not have been the surprise in part of her they had got the killer so soon, the manpower and attention like no case before it. Yet disappointment weighed inside her. The victory was sealed elsewhere before Juliet contributed to it. The climax was less thrilling, less monumental than she could have predicted. Doubt still plagued her, yet the government's willingness to read the alleged offender's mind diluted the concern.

"Take me outside?" Juliet quizzed after a moment of continued silence.

"I don't think you should."

"Let's go anyway," Juliet said, swallowing the last of her coffee and scanning up and down the corridor in search of an exit sign.

The walk was a silent affair. There was something on Tom's mind and Juliet knew it was brewing, threatening to spill out. As he offered his sheepskin coat to cover Juliet's gown she complied without objection and let whatever was to come happen. Outside, the early morning was cool, the air light and clear as it filled Juliet's lungs. Summer would turn into autumn before too long, and with it the light, early mornings would disappear.

"I'm going to request a transfer," Tom said after a long inhale of air. "Once you're back on your feet."

The words took Juliet by surprise, something of a rarity with her ability. A clanging headache, fatigue and the general battering were taking their toll.

"It's something I've been mulling over a while, even before this case," Tom continued. "I think it'd be good for both of us."

Somewhat stunned, Juliet's follow-up took a second. "So what's the plan? Go back to being a frustrated detective?"

"Frustrated maybe," Tom acknowledged, sweeping an arm in front of him. "But as a detective, at least I knew my place in all this."

"Is it because of what happened with Mike?"

"Maybe it's an age thing, a midlife crisis of sorts. I look back on why I joined the force in the first place. I was an idealist at heart. I believed in the police, I still do, that the uniform and institution meant something more than the individuals who wore it. To protect people in their own lives, uphold the rule of law and maybe, just maybe, leave the country in a better place than what I inherited. As a detective, reality tainted that optimism. Too long spent in case files of murders, rapes and violent crime. I needed something bigger, hope, and then you came along."

For a moment Juliet stared forward, out at the hospital car park and the far beyond green. "I'm not sure what you want me to say," she finally stated. "Do you want me to convince you not to transfer, to continue working with me?"

"I think we're way past that," Tom confirmed, a saddened tone in his voice. "This has been coming a while."

"The end of an era," Juliet smiled, though the tension in the air was not one of pleasant nostalgia.

"Why do you do it, Juliet?" Tom asked, the bitterness clear. "The actions that move beyond the acceptable line."

Bandaged up, black and blue from bruises, Juliet tried to joke the statement away. "Sometimes it happens to me, you know?"

"I mean it, Juliet," Tom stated. "Nearly a decade we've worked together, yet now and then, when I finally think I understand you, something comes out the woodwork to surprise me."

"What happened with Mike shouldn't have surprised you," Juliet replied. "I will do everything I can to solve a case. Even if that means stepping over the line."

"And what about the cost of it?" Tom pressed. "Say they pull you off the case, you never work with Ethan again. What then? You'll have forced yourself into a place where you can't help anymore."

"I can read minds, Tom," Juliet responded. "There's never a case of this size they won't want me involved in."

"Are you sure about that? What about Will Bowman?"

Will Bowman, the reason for the distance in the last year between Juliet and Tom. The case that had changed everything. Hayley Wilson, a girl no older than five, was taken from her mum in a park. They interviewed witnesses, checked CCTV and scrutinised the local sex offenders list to no progress. Twenty-four hours turned into a week, which turned into two, and everyone involved in the case knew it was a body they were looking for. The girl was impossibly cute, her image haunting the front pages of newspapers. Freckles, enormous auburn eyes and a smile in every photo. Joy. Juliet looked at this girl and knew she was somebody who brought joy to all those around her.

"I became obsessed with it. I couldn't sleep knowing this kid was out there. Usually I slept just fine, but something about those innocent eyes drew me in too deep," Juliet admitted. "But you tell a member of the public what I did, nine out of ten would accept it."

"And what evidence do we have that he did it, Juliet?" Tom questioned. "Bar your account, how do we know Will was responsible? How do we know your actions were justice against the right person?"

Bowman was the man brought in and fitted up by the police. A cleaner at the nursery Hayley attended most mornings. It had to be somebody Hayley knew and trusted, or there would have been a scene. He'd been giving the detectives nothing, an iron defence and his house, car and place of work said nothing either. To the untrained eye, he was clean, so they sent Juliet in to be sure. As soon as she saw the suspect Juliet knew, spotting an instinct and a darkness in Bowman's eyes.

"We found the body, right?"

Anything mentioned in the interview drew a blank. Bowman knew the girl and recognised her, but there was nothing violent and nothing sexual in his thoughts. That's when the image of Hayley kept popping up in her head. Juliet saw this guy sat there, an almost self-satisfied look on his face.

"You dug deeper than you should. People's brains are wired tight and the longer you were in there, the more pressure he was under. You squeezed him until he soiled his pants, and he was verbally unresponsive. Well, your instinct was right, and the police gained the location of the body. But at what cost Juliet?"

"Are you forgetting he tried to burn the body and chopped her limbs off? A body so charred up the parents couldn't identify it as little Hayley. They had to use dental records."

"And yet Will Bowman was still innocent until proved guilty. The evidence of a body gained when the suspect became temporarily comatose meant nothing. The entire case was about to be thrown out, the man walking free. So while he's sat there in court, you went a step further than mind-reading. Didn't you?"

"I get in his head right there and then in court. No digging this time, I carve right in and dump that image in the front and centre of that sick fuck's head."

Tom's face darkened. He knew what was coming next.

"It meant he couldn't bury her face. Every object reminded him of her, every face created that image of the burnt-out body and it twisted him up inside. Couldn't sleep, couldn't eat. A week later he hanged himself in his cell."

"You murdered him, Juliet," Tom stated. "You forced a man to kill himself and I lied to protect you."

"It was justice," Juliet insisted.

"Revenge," Tom replied firmly. "One potential child murderer got what he deserved, but what was the cost?"

"There was no *potential* about it," was Juliet's retort. "How else did he know where the body was?"

"We'll never know," Tom confirmed. "Because he killed himself before any court case could finish or due process could take place. Just because you can read a man's mind, doesn't know you know the man."

"I brought Will Bowman down when the justice system was about to fail," Juliet answered.

"What did Hayley's parents think? Did you ever read their minds to find out?"

Juliet's face momentarily flushed beet-red. "If you felt so

passionately about it, why lie?"

"My sin to own," Tom admitted. "I could have killed your career, but what would I have achieved? Robbed the world of what it had left to gain of a special talent? I believe in redemption, second chances. Watching you burn out into nothing would have been a waste."

"So you made the same judgement I did," Juliet confirmed. "You broke the rules for your own interpretation of right and wrong."

"True," Tom agreed. "But I will not be a part of it again. I believe in the justice system, every right and every wrong within it. I can't be complicit in eroding its core again."

"What I did with John's father wasn't the same," Juliet insisted.

"Wasn't it? Mike may have gone away and gathered us a piece of information that helped the case," Tom explained. "But you told a vulnerable individual he had failed as a father and his dead son was a drug addict. Until the day he dies, that knowledge is a part of him. Who were you to judge and who were you to decide?"

Juliet remained silent for a considerable length of time as Tom offered nothing further. She willed him to move, but he looked at her with his mind blank.

"The power you have to read minds, it's special," Tom mulled aloud. "Whatever comes next for you, all I ask is don't abuse it. Don't waste it. Used in the right way, it's a force for good, far more than anybody like me can ever offer. Continue down this wrong path and the public out there will fear it."

Chapter Twelve

"The drink is killing you," the doctor stated, his voice grave and accompanied with judgement. In a gown stripped of any dignity, Mike had awoken in a hospital bed. There'd been another collapse, a blackout, and once again another doctor, another face he'd forget, gave him familiar advice. The medical world had long ago stopped begging Mike, only resigned advice left to offer. Over the years, Mike had discarded the pamphlets he'd received a thousand times. The meetings, the stories, and the advice meant well. But such advice held little sway with Mike. He didn't want their help.

How long had it been since John died, since the events in London? Days, weeks, a month? Mike could no longer say. The drink robbed time, any anchoring to it or memory of it. One drink followed another, and by god had he hit the bottle hard.

In London, Mike had awoken to the sound of a police officer's voice. Curled up on a park bench, head banging and wearing a suit, the officer had asked him if he was okay. Mike explained he wasn't, that he was John Fitzgerald's father and that in the chaos at the eulogy he had become separated from his escort. The officer radioed, and it wasn't long before a car picked him up. A distraught Charlotte met him at a police station, apologising for losing him. Mike explained it wasn't the young lady's fault. Charlotte explained in return that there had been an accidental gunshot, a crush and injured people. She thought he might have been one of them.

More figures appeared, more senior than Charlotte. The black man introduced as the senior investigating officer offered his joy first. The delight was bright in his eyes; Ethan, if Mike remembered his name correctly.

"We got him," he said, a firm hand landing on Mike's shoulder. "We got the bastard that killed your son."

A sea of beaming faces, gritted teeth and vengeful smiles. Mike could not join them in their pleasure. As they moved away, the floor beneath Mike fell away, his knees crumpled like he had heard the news all over again and he clenched a hand to his chest. Faces blurred, and the surroundings softened. Mike's eyes opened again only when he was in a hospital. That was the first time. A handful since.

The face of John's killer, a mugshot from a previous stint in prison, sat front and centre of every channel. A scrawny man, gaunt features with greasy, wiry hair stared back at him. A face ugly and yellowed. Broken teeth and gums. The face of Casper Smith was one you didn't want to look at for too long. The man didn't look like a murderer; he looked like the man huddled in a sleeping bag you flicked your eyes away from as he begged for change. A person who had slipped off the edge of the surface, Mike found himself hard-pressed to hate the face before him. Maybe it's because he saw himself in the expression too. Part of him wanted a pantomime villain, an evil face that encouraged revulsion. A foreign world leader or conspiracy would have been easier to stomach. But just as the killing was amateurish, so was its artist. Mike could barely believe it had ended so cheaply.

After a full night's rest, followed by some blood samples and swabs, the doctors and Charlotte said Mike could go – there was a chauffeur-driven car to take him home. Talk of the court case, and a public funeral fell on empty ears. Mike just wanted to go home.

On his return Mike entered a tidy house, as the police officer had promised, with a fully stocked fridge thrown in. Almost as soon as Mike had reached London, he was on his way back the same way, Charlotte's business card and his house keys in his pocket.

For countless days Mike hit the drink hard. As if out of practice, he tore through whatever he could get his hands on. Pale ales to whiskey to bottles of wine in a sitting. Every few drinks he'd crawl to the toilet, sometimes not even that far, and empty his stomach in time for another round. Curtains drawn, the poisons flowed through him. Between the drink there was sleep and scraping together of meals, but Mike quickly forgot what life without hangovers and headaches felt like.

Segregating himself alone in his squalor, the television stayed switched off, knocks at the door went unanswered, and he had ripped the phone out of the wall. Bitterness, anger and a mean, animalistic hatred brewed inside Mike, who wanted nothing more than to suffer in dark isolation.

After what could have been two or three days, Mike stopped giving a fuck; counting the resentment of his own thoughts was losing its edge, but the need to be angry hadn't subsided. The thing about mental self-harm was eventually the triggers became blunt and fresh instruments were necessary to produce the same fury.

In the hallway of his house there were photos, talismans and knickknacks everywhere. From an outside perspective, it was all cheap tat but there was a story behind it all – personal and historical slices of a time gone by. Planting his feet in a house he'd walked for decades, Mike tried to look at it all with fresh eyes.

A tour of Mike's home was more like a museum than a house. Sporting medals, holiday photos and report cards all hung from the walls as a living monument to a boy always destined for greatness. Whether boxing, rugby or running, the boy was the best at whatever he tried. With the intensity, drive and discipline he'd instilled in his son no matter what, he'd eventually be the best. But the boy commemorated by his father was not the son people would expect – it was David, rather than John, whose life plastered the walls.

As Mike worked the walls, reminiscing about fishing trips, walks and sporting events, the absence of John grew larger with every step. A stranger trying to learn about Mike would picture one son, not two, as if a deliberate attempt had been to erase John from existence. Yet as Mike studied his surroundings, he justified himself to an invisible witness. Mike loved *both* his sons, there was no favourite or preferred child.

Sickness had come and robbed him of David. Short, powerful and blunt, the illness had consumed David and rotted his body inside and out. No matter how good a mentor Mike had been, regardless of how driven and capable his son had become, the disease had no care who it targeted. But Mike had never loved one more than the other, had he? Maybe he had designed the shrine to the son he lost, and that explained the mismatch.

But Marco's words rang in Mike's ears.

That was the kind of man he was.

The words from Marco's story haunted him. Was Mike deluding himself, blocking out the reality? Parenting solo had been hard, diminishing and difficult to get right, but he'd loved those boys, fathered and mentored them as best he could. The comments had echoed and bounced in his brain for days. Rattled each time they repeated, Mike silently raged further. Yet there were still no signs of John.

Pulling his glasses from his eyes, Mike leant back in his seat and tried to remember. His brain rattled for recollection, but something clouded the memories in fog. Angry, drunk and bitter. So many of those years were a blur where he felt like he was in the passenger seat rather than in control.

From what he could recall, Mike remembered fondly what it was like to be a mentor, to have the attention of two inexperienced boys who clung on every word. Like every father-son relationship, there came a time where the boy would ask the man for advice. Bullies at school had been stealing John's lunch, pushing him over and humiliating him in front of his classmates. The teacher's advice had been to tell them, but Mike had raised no snitch. They earned respect and in the background, on the quiet, he advised John to fight back, to take a beating if he must.

Two days later John returned home sobbing, the mud on his clothes and grazes on his skin visible. Mike had waited outside his door, listened to the weeping, but felt nothing but pride. The stories of bullying stopped and as a father, he felt his work was complete. Had the guidance driven the boy to hate him? The purpose was to build resolve within his son, to strengthen, not weaken him.

Mike unscrewed the cap from the wine and took another

deep swig from the bottle. It fucked his head, his mind all over the place. David had always made sense, always been the good older child made in his image, whereas John had been the outlier. When Mike said left, John went right; when Mike pushed him in a direction, it only made John drift further away.

That was the kind of man he was. The statement was stirring him up like crazy. Somewhere in his thoughts, Mike had grabbed a ladder and was halfway up, intending to reach the attic. The crawlspace over his head was a museum of trash that slowly revealed itself. Over several years, anything in the way got shoved out of sight rather than cleared. Forget the hallway pictures, the truth would lie up in the darkness.

The space lit by a cheap torch, Mike hauled himself up after quite a struggle, getting too old for such exertion. The expected junk was up here: broken toys, prams and discarded clothes in trunks. As Mike sorted through the jumble, it scared him that nothing triggered any memories. Most of the possessions up here were ones he'd have bought himself with Maggie out of the picture, yet they stimulated nothing. Baby clothes, toddler outfits, school uniforms and toys all drew a blank reaction. Had those heavy drinking days clouded so much?

After much searching Mike came across a box, tucked into the corner which caught his eye. This time he knew exactly what it would be, and his heart sank in his chest. Yet his hand grabbed it and brought it down with him. The family photo album that nobody had updated since the day Maggie passed.

In it were heart-breaking amounts of empty pages; Mike never had the urge to take many photos after Maggie. As he sat flicking through, images of a happy family greeted him. A beaming baby and panting toddler with a proud mother and father behind. Never much money but always the best they could muster – there were walks, picnics and small trips to the beach littered in there.

The last photo was of Mike beaming, a smile he couldn't recognise. In one photo a toddler David stuck out his tongue and in the other John looked utterly confused and lost. Better times, simpler and happier. Months later, those boys would be motherless and Mike left alone to parent them.

It was the absence that hurt the most.

The wine bottle smashed against the wall, and Mike swept the album to the floor. Drunk and furious, Mike had found an unfamiliar method by which to torture himself. Yet as he staggered back towards the ladder, his eyes fell onto an open page in the album – a barbeque with other adults who had kids of their own. Who were they? Then it clicked.

Mike knew where he needed to go.

Hammering on the door, Mike could see no light on inside. Would she even still live there? Rage and stubbornness meant he rejected any possibility of that not being the case. Besides, who born and raised in Bellington really got out? Through darkened streets he'd stumbled, along pavements and paths not walked in over a decade. With his memory, was he even getting it right? Finally he came upon a place that matched up with his memory; now dark, it was hard to trace whether the comparison he was making was accurate.

"LINDA!" Mike bellowed. "LINDA HUGHES."

Somewhere to the side a light flicked on and the curtains of an upstairs window twitched. At the window was a woman in her fifties, with dyed brown hair and squinting eyes. Right street, wrong house. He was sure that was Linda.

"LINDA!" Mike yelled as he stumbled over front walls in the

window's direction. Progress was slow over such hurdles, but still Mike kept leaping.

"SHUT THE HELL UP, SOME OF US HAVE JOBS IN THE MORNING," an angry voice yelled from an unknown window.

The front door was thrown open, light spilling out into the night. A woman in a dressing gown appeared and Mike fell to her feet. Staring down at him was a stern and unwelcoming expression he hadn't crossed paths with in years. The face he pictured in his mind was younger. Had it all really had been that long ago? Hands on hips, Linda did not look happy.

"Mike? Jesus Christ, it's half eleven at night," the woman squinted down and spat. "What the hell are you doing here? Someone will call the police."

Sobbing on the floor, Mike's chosen words neither came out in the intended order nor made much sense. "Heroin in my boy. They found heroin in him, Linda. It's all my fault."

"Get inside," Linda spat again as she half-dragged, half-helped Mike through the front door.

Linda pulled Mike to a chair where the room spun around him. The sound of a kettle boiling, smacking porcelain and cupboards being thrown open echoed around him.

Slamming a large jug of water on the table before him along with a glass, Linda ordered him to drink. "We don't even speak until that's looking empty. If I'm even to give you two minutes of my time, I want Michael Fitzgerald to be coherent and sober."

Mike murmured a response, and with little accuracy poured himself a drink. Linda joined him sternly across the table and true to her word remained silent as she watched him swallow back water. A cigarette and a coffee. It was nearly twenty minutes, and her second cigarette stubbed into an ashtray, before she finally deemed him to have drunk enough.

"You keep going," she instructed. "What is it you want, Mike?"

His head spinning considerably less, Mike focused on Linda. A former neighbour, she had regularly babysat for the boys in the early years before moving across town. Maggie became close with her, confided in and bonded with her. Mike was never high on her approval list. Why had he wanted to see her? Where else could the boy have received enough help to stay away? No friends, no family and seventeen. The boy should have come crawling back. He didn't, and that required help.

"I need to know where the boy went after he ran away," Mike stammered. "He'd have come here, whether he got your help or not – this would have been one of the few places he knew he would be welcome."

"I expected you over fifteen years ago," Linda chided. "He came here, crying his eyes out and in a state. You had beaten him again and said some unforgivable things. He begged me to make sure he never had to go back. I watched a teenage boy at rock bottom *beg* for an escape. I told him there was always a bed here for him. He said he needed to go further, as far away as he could. So I gave him all I had in cash, two hundred pounds, and the next morning he got a bus out of here. I never saw him in person again, aside from on the news, just like you must have done. But you know all that. So why did it take you fifteen years to give a flying fuck about your son, Mike?"

Mike swallowed some more water. "He was better off without me. The longer I left it, the more I knew he must have been okay."

"A nice excuse to shift the responsibility but you're right, he was better off without you," Linda snapped. The years had not softened the anger in her eyes or fury in her tone. "Do you even remember what you told him? I will answer that myself so you don't manipulate it. You told your youngest son you wished it was him that had died, not Maggie or David. After all that boy had been through, what kind of monster were you?"

Mike had no excuses left. Had he really said that? Time had wiped the memory of the words, only leaving faint remembrance of the outcome. Nothing surprised him anymore; the chilling anxiety and bitterness in his body after a drink a permanent fixture. Internally he told himself that he hadn't meant it, he loved the child but there was that side to him that clamoured to hurt others as much as itself. Racist slurs, homophobia or many evil taunts had left his lips in the past, anything to twist the knife enough to tear a reaction out of the kindest of souls.

"After what happened with Maggie and the cancer, David and his sickness, I let myself self-destruct. I'm sorry every day that John was around for that."

"Sorry every day? Are you even listening to yourself? There was no sickness for David, he killed himself. Hanged himself in your own home," Linda said, shaking with fury. "Tell yourself he was ill, tell anyone who cares to listen that a rapid sickness took him away. Absolve yourself of any blame, but deep down I know you remember the truth. You had two boys who needed a man and a father to step up to the plate. Instead, they had you. You pushed and you pushed those boys, until both of them snapped."

The sensation was like Mike was falling without the ground in sight. His stomach turned and his body felt light. Of course he remembered what had happened to David: suicide, two years older than John, he hadn't coped well with the loss of his mother. To fill the void Mike had poured attention into him, be it sporting or school success, hoping it would be enough to pull him through. Hindsight was a wonderful thing. The warning signs were all there, yet Mike had missed them. There was no coming back after the moment they lowered the casket of his first-born son into the ground.

"When you and Maggie were first married, we used to joke that there was the truth and then your amended version. We used to mock the alternative reality in your head, one where you could never not be the hero. It wasn't a gag though, it went deeper than that, didn't it? You can't even separate the truth from the lie anymore – you aren't even sure yourself."

Linda laughed when Mike offered no response. "Why are you even here, Mike? On a holiday in your own past? A tourist in your youth? Let me tell you how I really feel now Maggie nor the boys are in earshot. I told her to leave you a hundred times. I had begged her to. But Maggie, bless her heart, stayed torn between her love for you and the chaos that came with it. Then she found a lump, cancer, and any resilience she had crumbled. It was swift, too far along, and it was an injustice in this world that such a wonderful woman like her died and you stayed behind. One look at you and I can see all the torture and pain you have endured over the years, but it still can't make me happy, not after all you inflicted on that poor innocent family."

"Anything you say I can't disagree with," Mike admitted. "I was a terrible husband, a worse father, a drunk and a violent one at that. I'm not here for forgiveness, sympathy or some kind of redemption. I'm here because I want to know the truth about the boy and I can't even answer you why. Maybe it will make it seem all worth it? That he turned out okay despite all my influence? Maybe it is a selfish trip. I will die soon, every inch of my body is screaming at me to stop with the drinking, but I know that if I stop the rest of me does too, it runs too deep these days. You don't owe me anything, but what do you know about the boy?"

Another cigarette was lit as Linda, hands shaking with rage, smoked. There was a decade of hatred in her body. Her face winced and curled up in some kind of revulsion every time her eyes even flicked at Mike.

"He wrote me a letter a year or two later," Linda confirmed. "All you need to know is that he was okay. He landed nowhere worse than he did that night. He seemed happy."

A wave of relief washed over Mike before being replaced. The boy had run away from home, ended in a place safe far from Mike. A soldier and eventually a superhero. Yet the idea he landed nowhere worse was a falsehood. Somewhere heroin came into the mix.

"They let me see the body. He had heroin in his bloodstream," Mike said, his voice cracking. "He was an addict and any idea he died okay is a lie. I need to know what happened."

Concern grew in Linda's face. She could see no lie in Mike's face, but she remained cautious, hostile. "What do you want from me?"

Mike shrugged awkwardly. "I came here because you were the next logical step in the story; I guess what I need to know is where he ended up next. At some point he joined the army and after that flew into the sky. Outside of those sketchy details, I don't know a thing. And I want to. It's too late to make amends now, but I want to know what happened to my son."

Linda shifted in her seat and took another drag on her cigarette. "I don't think John was ever in the army."

It was Mike's turn to survey Linda and see no lie in her face.

"What makes you say that?"

Linda got to her feet. "I'm showing you this for him, not you."

Leaving the room, Mike heard boxes being opened in the next room as he finished his water. A few minutes passed by and Linda returned with a sheet of paper.

"Two years later he sent me this letter as a thank you. I saved it because the words were kind and it meant something, even after all this time. I will let you read it, only so you can get a sense of what I mean."

"Read it."

"What?"

"I can't read, Linda."

"You're joking."

When Mike said nothing, Linda laughed and shook her head. "That makes sense now. A violent man who could never express what was going on in his head in words. How does that even happen?"

"They kept telling me I'd get it," Mike replied, embarrassed. "Yet the years went by and I never did. It was like reading Chinese. Eventually school was just about surviving. I was in fights, I was defiant, I was a clown, I was a disruptor and eventually I got expelled. After that I went down the pits with my dad and uncle. I didn't need words after that."

Linda paused as if absorbing a new side to Mike. It made his eyes look down, but her stare remained in place. Eventually she got whatever she was after, nodded, and Mike was secretly thankful she resisted mocking further.

Dear Linda,

For nearly two years I've begun this letter, but never quite found the words that seemed right to finish it. I can only say I'm sorry for that. You told me to let you know when I was safe, but I selfishly delayed doing so. Enclosed you'll find every penny of the two hundred pounds you gave me that night, and a little more. I know you'd say it wasn't about the money, that it was mine to keep, but pride meant I felt I owed you it back someday. This letter is to let you know I'm not just safe, but doing better than that.

I can never repay you the true amount I owe you for what you did that night, but I hope this update lets you know just how important it was and my future. I live in Leeds now, have my flat and a job. None of it is fancy – I work nights as a cleaner hoovering office blocks and emptying bins. But I love it all, and it's mine. For the first time in my life, I can honestly say I've carved out something of my own. I'm putting myself through college to get qualifications that hopefully means I can have something better-paid someday. None of it's really a plan, but I'm planting seeds for the future, making sure I have as many options as I can.

I hope you are well and that this letter hasn't come too late. The last thing I wanted was to have you worrying about the last couple of years. I needed enough space and distance to start afresh and hopefully the small paragraphs show how much you helped me. To repeat what I said earlier, I can never repay you enough. I wish I had the confidence to deliver this in person, but Bellington still brings back too many evil memories for me. If I am ever in the area, I will knock on your door and thank you properly in person.

I hope you are well and that we meet again soon. Thank you for everything.

John

Putting down the letter, Linda allowed Mike to let the words sink in for a moment. Leeds and a job as a cleaner. Somebody who Mike didn't recognise, a quiet voice that was happy, wrote the letter. Yet this wasn't the story that Mike knew, not the tale the media had told. Why the difference?

"They said he joined the army at eighteen," Linda interjected. "I've checked that several times. His military record is all up there online. But John wrote this letter at nineteen – there's not even a hint of the military on there. I don't know why, but I think the government or John made it up later."

"Have you ever told anyone else?"

"My loyalty was to him and will continue to be," Linda assured. "But if you're to follow his story once he left here, a stint in the army is not the place to go. Leeds is the place to look."

Mike sat back in his seat. Why would the government and media lie? A cover-up? If John wasn't in the military in those interim years, where was he?

"Did you ever see him again, after that night?"

For years Mike thought about reaching out, going for a coffee or a sandwich, but never did. There was always an excuse ready: he'd be too busy, it'd do more harm than good or that he'd not reply. The dilemma was one that felt like it would outlast Mike rather than John. The longer time went on, the less a reunion made sense.

When Mike did not answer, Linda could only shake her head. "I've given up trying to understand how men like you work," she sighed. "It's obvious – pick up the phone, stop drinking, just stop trying to destroy yourself for no reason, but you know that and I do. The ideal time to make amends was any time in the past ten years. Now the moment has passed."

"For what it's worth, I'm thankful for what you've shared with me tonight," Mike admitted as he finished his water and rose to his feet. "You owed me nothing."

Linda stayed sat at the table. Since the revelation about the illiteracy, her eyes had taken on a different look to the one that greeted him when he first entered. "I think you were a nasty piece of work Mike – whatever your demons there's no excuse for what you did to those boys and Maggie. For a decade I've wanted to give you a piece of my mind. I saw you cross roads to avoid me or bury your head in shame. But now I'm here, it's not all it lived up to be. You look ill, Mike, sick. You've killed yourself enough over it all."

"I'm not after anyone to save me," Mike said as he left. "I want to find out about my boy."

Chapter Thirteen

Her generation's Lee Harvey Oswald, John Wilkes Booth, or Gavrilo Princip. The man who murdered a superhero sat before Juliet. Would they ever know how much the world's future had changed due to one person's actions? Yet the figure of Casper Smith didn't seem notable, a face not destined to be in the history books or one that had shaken every government the world over.

Mousy hair, long and tangled, hung over Casper's eyes, occasionally swept away with a timid hand to reveal even more nervous eyes. A lawyer sat beside him, a portly fellow who was court-appointed. With no money to his name, no lawyer wanted to stake their reputation on somebody so reviled. Already the whispers were that Casper planned to plead guilty early, not let the situation escalate to trial and thus face further damnation in the media. A drug addict with an extensive conviction list of theft and shoplifting, there weren't any allies left for the man opposite.

For Juliet the eulogy resulted in three broken ribs, and a fractured left wrist – a lucky escape. After another day, she could return home for some rest and, cooped up inside, away from work, she found herself bored. The shower water stung every cut and slice on her body, and Juliet clenched her teeth through the pain. She would repair, it'd take just a little time. Keen to get back to work, her first task was to meet with John Fitzgerald's alleged killer.

Part of the interview was to show a willingness of the client to make amends. Already the evidence pointed to a botched killing, a manslaughter that was unplanned rather than a trained assassin. Yet other mysteries remained, even now they had their killer. The drugs in the system, how John came to be in a rough end of town that fateful night, and the biggest unknown of all relating to how his abilities stopped working. Extensive blood tests and autopsies on anyone with abilities did not establish a link, or even a hint at some explanation. Already scientists ruled the heroin out of the equation for stopping the regenerative abilities, even in its large quantities.

"What do you remember about the night he died?" Juliet asked as softly and tactfully as she could. There was little need for proof anymore.

Casper, his skin pale like paper, looked nervous and worn. The file before Juliet described him being thirty years old, but realistically he looked over forty. Homelessness and drug abuse had taken their toll, a shadow hanging permanently in his eyes and words as he spoke. In his mind his thoughts were frantic, skipping and hard to pin down. Running low on both sleep and withdrawing from the drugs he usually relied on, Casper had spent the last night in fear. Fellow prisoners were heckling at him, and was therefore being kept separate. Even the worst criminals had time for John Fitzgerald. He saved lives.

"For the past two years spice and heroin have been all I've chased," Casper slurred as his eyes stared into Juliet's shoulder rather than her face. "You'd know what it is better than me, but it works and it works so well my life has been skipping from one high to the next. I don't remember what happened in between."

"So you don't remember killing him?"

Casper scratched his chest. "All I remember is waking up in hospital. They found me covered in blood and presumed someone had stabbed me. Turned out it wasn't mine. It was his. They say I killed him."

Juliet stared at the dull eyes before her for any sense of a lie. "And do you think you killed him?"

Casper shrugged. "It's a blur. I remember lashing out, maybe with a bottle at someone. It's where all the evidence points, spice makes you... me, violent and if I felt cornered or provoked it's probably what went down. I guess you're wanting to know how I did it? Well, it won't have been my doing."

Juliet looked towards the glass with desperate eyes. Not a lie in his voice or a fib in his mind. The killer before Juliet was as much a part of the death of John Fitzgerald as the broken glass bottle. No memory of the event, the culprit answered for, the why now redundant but the how far from becoming clear.

The face-to-face chat lasted ten minutes as Juliet breezed through every nook and cranny of the story. Police suspected John had confronted a drug-induced Casper attempting to break into a car. In a panic and with rising hostility, Casper had fled down an alleyway only to come face to face again with John again. High on drugs and in a bleak area, Casper found the nearest object he could, a bottle, and had vague recollections of smashing it against a wall before repeatedly stabbing someone with it. Only as he woke up the next day, covered in blood, did he have absent recollections of the night before.

Slender in frame, clothes hanging off the body, Casper was an unremarkable figure. The truth beneath the surface, however, would become apparent to even the most untrained of eyes. Casper's eyes were a little too wide as they rested, intense and forever flicking. A void lay slightly behind the mask as Juliet saw an individual broken and crazed by years of drug abuse. The toll they'd taken was clear in his speech and mental health, as through rotting teeth he stumbled over simple sentences and ideas.

"How could this man have killed John Fitzgerald?" Juliet stated to Ethan upon exiting the interview. With a certainty she knew that he had, the face that lingered in the mind was that of Lee Harvey Oswald. An unassuming-looking man whose actions would transcend and define the era they lived in.

"DNA evidence, a motive, and a full confession," Ethan beamed, the relief in his body language obvious. "We solved the case, Juliet, we've done our job. We caught the killer."

"Don't you care about how?" Juliet exclaimed. "How one day John can go from deflecting bullets to dying from stab wounds?"

"That's not my job, Juliet," Ethan confirmed. "They asked me to catch the killer, and that's exactly what I have done, in just over a day."

"Just like the rest of them," Juliet scorned, unheard as she stalked away. Ethan had been no different from the other detectives of the past, like Tom, obsessed with the system. The truth or pursuing a crime all the way to its conclusion, was an alien concept for those in the field. Police cracking down on easy wins to hit arrest numbers, prosecutors dropping risky cases in desperation to hit conviction targets, and detectives doing the bare minimum to 'solve' a case. A numbers game, the victims forgotten, the truth irrelevant.

Tom had left sooner than either of them expected following the hospital visit, a new partner not yet assigned. Until then Juliet had requested some annual leave, to recover from her injuries and get back into shape. Helen Becton, the head of Juliet's branch of employment, approved it herself.

That was how Juliet came to find herself outside Middleton Court for the first time in two years. Sat in her rented car, Juliet had been in the car park for over ten minutes. The drive had been a continuous one from London, with little traffic and most of the day ahead of her. The grounds of the hall were beautiful and in bloom, a well-maintained path around the complex and a pond sat before her, the water shining in the summer sun. They forecasted it to be a scorcher. Yet Juliet willed herself to be anywhere else in the world.

A part of Juliet hoped that the message at the desk would be that he was on a day trip. Juliet decided not to ring ahead. Yet he didn't really go on day trips in recent years. The wheelchair and lack of mobility made such outings a burden for the staff. The home was no poor existence. A purpose-built nursing home for those requiring top levels of individual care, friendly, professional staff provided the patient-centred nursing care. There was a high ratio of staff to residents. All this Juliet had read in the pamphlet many years ago and picked this one. The government covered the bill.

One step at a time Juliet pulled herself out of the car and in the reception's direction. Her reaction was laughable, like a child nervous as they entered a new school year, yet the anxiety was thick and real. This was outside of her comfort zone.

"Graham Reynolds?" Juliet asked softly to the lady at front desk. "Which is his room?"

"Down the hall and on the right-hand side, past the dining room," came the soft, smiling reply.

As Juliet tensed, she began the lengthy walk down the corridors. The retirement home was still; those she passed, whether beaming nurses or delicate residents, took their time with every step. Little need to rush in an environment with no deadlines.

During the drive, repeatedly, Juliet had imagined a knock and a nervous wait for a response. Yet when she reached her father's door it was open, propped by a dog doorstop. Inside the room, it looked just as it had done in her memories. The furniture cut out of his bungalow home and pasted here in an alien room. White walls and cream carpets did little to blend with dark wooden furniture built for another life, time and place.

The day he moved in came flooding back. The bungalow sold and any furniture not following Graham to the home sold with it. Her father had sobbed and begged not to leave, even after the sale. The old man had gripped her softly but as hard as he could muster on the sleeves. *Please,* his wide eyes willed with fear. He'd been found wandering in a dressing gown in the middle of the night, the forgetfulness getting worse and losing ability to even cook a proper meal. All the reasons were logical, but logic proved no answer to a man saying goodbye to his independence forever.

Old then, and even older now. Her father was more fragile than Juliet could have once ever pictured him. On a comfy chair in the corner, a glaze to his eyes, they stared before him, his hands resting on his lap in a warm jumper and cord trousers. A pair of cosy slippers covered feet that had long since lost the ability to support him. Mouth agape to the point of drooling, Juliet flicked her eyes elsewhere. Anywhere.

Shame dragged Juliet like a magnet towards her father. His eyesight had never been the best, and his senses were so dulled that it was only as she was right on top of him he realised he had a visitor.

"Dad," she whispered as she gripped his hands, internally wincing at how cold they felt in spite of his warm room.

Head and eyes slowly moving to focus on the face before him, Graham raised a frail hand and stroked the side of her face. "Jane?" was the restful spoken word as his mouth stretched into a smile.

"Your daughter, Juliet," she corrected. The words were unaccompanied by an unexpected tremble.

The face of Juliet's father remained glazed. No thoughts stirred in response to her voice or name. The smile remained, however. *Jane,* he thought over and over. *Jane.*

To pull away, Juliet grabbed a jug of water from the side, filling a glass. Raising it to her father's lips, he gladly sipped it down. The silence was as it was last time as Juliet spoke. She made small talk about the weather and the home. Graham couldn't grip onto her words anymore. He hadn't been able to for a long time.

With his thoughts loose and thin, Juliet did the talking for both of them. She told him about her life, her job, and the comings and goings with the John Fitzgerald case. Words stirred and developed in his head occasionally, recognition mostly. Words and sounds associated with long-forgotten moments fizzled to the surface before bubbling away a second later.

"I was thinking about Mum the other day," Juliet smiled before adding, "Jane."

"Jane," Graham replied with a distant look in his eyes. "My beautiful wife."

"I was looking in the mirror and I reminded myself of her. Younger, like a photo that hung on the wall as a child. We never looked much alike, you and I, but I look back now and realise what a miniature version of her I was and still am. It's funny how that works."

Graham nodded along with Juliet's words, the association comforting. Her voice he recognised all right, her face sparking familiarity too. But like an object floating on the surface, the memory of Juliet was no longer rooted to anything solid – ever present but detached from the familiar day to day.

Twelve years ago, it still felt so recent, but one look at her father reminded her how long ago it must have been. Once he had been strong, stern and a stable figure in her life. Conservative in both political ideology and life outlook, he had been firm on her need to be a lady, marry and settle down to raise a family. Christianity had been equally important, a moral compass was what society sorely lacked, he said, and a church visit every Sunday morning kept the soul in check.

The news of her mother's cancer had been a formal sit-down, the head of the family informing the daughter of the news. No comfort, no hugs. Graham had stiffened in his chair awkwardly as Juliet wept. It was Jane with the cancer, not them. They needed to be stronger, to allow for her to be weaker. Juliet had drawn back the tears, buried the emotion and been the solid foundation necessary for her mother.

Yet cancer did not play according to any rules. It spread, and it had won. In the grief and the struggle afterwards, Juliet noticed a change within herself. Not the typical change that a sixteen-year-old went through, though there was that too. No, as Juliet isolated herself often in her room, alone in her own thoughts, she realised that she was accessing other people's too. Emotions at first, then snippets of words and the occasional sensation. No mother, a stern father, and an ability she had not yet understood since Juliet hid it from the world.

On her birthday, Graham took Juliet for dinner. A fine, youthful woman now, her father wished for her to experience a lifestyle a strong and successful marriage could bring her. Alongside the multi-course meal and the fine wine was a box, a beautiful purple wrapped square with a bow.

In the box was a cigar, a present from her father. The old man had loved them, a whisky and a cigar after dinner. The treats were his way of relaxing after a day in the city at work. Juliet recalled being sat at the table, fascinated, as her father watched as she twirled the cigar in her hand. After a moment he asked her, "Juliet, what country do you think makes the best cigars in the world?"

"Cuba," had been her answer after a moment's thought. Everyone knew Cuban cigars were the best in the world.

"Once," her father nodded with a smile. "Then there was the revolution in Cuba and the country became communist, of sorts, and the United States put the country under a trade embargo. You are a woman now, Juliet. If you make the best product in the world and make lots of money, but suddenly one day you cannot even sell your product, what do you do?"

"You move?" Juliet countered after a moment, pondering.

"Exactly," her father said with enthusiasm. "And that's what the cigar-making masters did. Some to Florida, many to the Dominican Republic. Using their influence and connections, they left Cuba and took their business elsewhere. Yet today, if I was to ask the average person on the street who made the world's best cigars, they would answer Cuba too. Even though for the past several decades, the masters that generated the reputation transferred elsewhere."

"But that makes little sense!" Juliet had exclaimed. "If you like cigars, you would buy the best cigars."

"That, Juliet, is the power of perception," her father had taught her. "Perception matters more to people than the reality. In your future career it is more important for your bosses to perceive you to be doing important work than carrying out the important work. In politics it is the party perceived as the most competent that gets elected, not the best party for the job. For Cuban cigars, it was the mystique of life behind an embargo, the taboo of smoking something illegal that ensured they could maintain the reputation. Actual cigar connoisseurs know that it is more of a brand than reality."

"So where do your cigars come from, Dad?" Juliet had quizzed.

"Cuba," her father laughed. "Sometimes it's fun to play along with what makes an enjoyable story."

The dinner ended, and the pair returned home. Before she fled upstairs, her father embraced in a rare hug. As he held her, told her how proud he was, he imagined his wife. Juliet looked like her, felt like her, and reminded him oh so much of her. Juliet was like a daily ghost to him, a haunting. And then the statement came. The one Juliet could never bury. *I wish it had been you.*

As the hug ended, her father had smiled and retreated to his room. Shocked and numb, Juliet had slowly done the same, questioning what she had heard inside his brain. A momentary lapse, an opinion never meant to be public. Yet for a moment it was real, and Juliet could never shake how often that feeling occurred inside him.

Over the next two years the relationship strained as drip by drip, she heard it all. A fragment here, a snatch of information there. Juliet had always known they never planned for her. Society had told a father in his mid-fifties and a mother in her forties they could never bear children, and that had been the end of any discussion regarding children. Yet a pregnancy did eventually happen. Doctors advised it was at substantial risk to her mother to continue with the birth. Stubbornness prevailed, her father believed it was against both God and nature to end a pregnancy when there was a family around to support one. So that was that, and nine months later Juliet emerged, a crying infant into the arms of parents who all her life would be mistaken as grandparents.

One day, near the end, there had been a hell of an argument and everything had all come out. Juliet revealed every dirty secret, every scornful nasty comment to a father shocked and pale. When the heat died down and the anger faded, Graham had done all he knew to do. He forced her to the doctors and after that, the police. Somehow the government cottoned on to investigate such a wild statement.

The pain Juliet felt as she looked into her father's eyes was too much. No amount of love, pride or strength of the bond could wipe the knowledge regarding the cracks in it all. There were statements that could never be taken back, should never have been considered. And that was the case with her father. He withheld his opinions. Yet she heard them anyway.

Before her, the once-formidable figure sat dazed and faded. The nurses had taken care of him, his clothes washed and clean, his hair combed and neat. The room was spotless and his face showed that his diet was far better than in the months before they brought him into care. She loved him and he loved her too, somewhere still in there at least. Yet the pain was still all there, right alongside.

As Juliet welled up at the image before her, knowing that her father was one of her last ties to the past, she jolted as he spoke.

"Everyone I know is going," he mumbled, his eyes momentarily wide. That's when she saw it, in his face more than anything. One by one, the residents of the home were dying off and a void taking their place. In comfort they slept, ate and existed, but in each of them there were the same overwhelming thoughts. Fear. Genuine fear and terror of what was to come next and doubt whether there was anything at all. That was all that Graham could anchor himself too. The reality that united everyone, even John. Graham knew he was old, soon to die, and this would be the last real place he would ever go.

Chapter Fourteen

On the day Mike buried his youngest son, there were no dramatic showers of rain or spectacular lightning storms. No icy breeze or hollow wind. For weeks Mike mapped out how he expected the day to proceed. In his mind he pictured winter, yet when the funeral finally came, reality bypassed every crafted idea.

The sky overhead held no clouds, and most would describe the temperature as warm. Rather than in darkness, the day passed in golden sunshine. There were crowds of faces in the distance, far from the actual events of the day. They filled the roads and streets for miles, a collective day of national mourning. Far from being the silent father at the graveside, Mike mourned in a sea of faces.

The government had paid for everything. Two days of mourning up and down the country filled the news. Just like the day of the murder, what felt like the entire world paused for reflection – a minute's silence for a lost hero. Wearing a black suit and tie, Mike pulled at the collar choking his neck. In the months to come, the discomfort remained his outstanding memory of the day.

The Bellington Church christened John and David at Maggie's insistence. Religion important to neither parent, the opportunity to celebrate in one event with friends and family became the primary motivation. Welcomed into the church with a sermon and hymns, the boys would, aside from school, never knowingly step foot into a place of worship again. No Christmas carols, no communion, no Sunday service.

Mike had a bottle of rum in his jacket to help calm his nerves and allow the events of the funeral to pass him by. His attention skipped mostly around the people present, around a hundred on what was very much a private occasion. The selective invite list reflected the opposite of the eulogy that erupted into chaos.

Regarding the attendees, Mike recognised the Prime Minister, but most of them he didn't. Some wept, the majority stood in stoic silence. The booze numbed Mike's senses enough that no tear or cry could leave his steel frame. The Reverend questioned whether Mike wished to say any words. The imagined scene of speeches, hollow words and gazing eyes frightened Mike into silence. The Lord's words would accompany the burial of his son. Words of meaning needed uttering a decade ago, their impact wasted now.

Mike felt like a watcher of another man's actions. A Union Jack was draped over the coffin, the events unravelling before his eyes signified the closing of a chapter. All the energy, the stories and the adventure of his son's life, existed as fragments in people's heads now. It was the third time Mike witnessed one of his family lowered into the ground. In a cruel twist of fate, he had become last man standing.

Refocusing on the ceremony, the Reverend went over to the coffin for what looked to be the last moments of the funeral. "Give him, o Lord, your peace and let your eternal light shine upon him."

"Amen," the congregation called.

Facing the congregation, the Reverend continued. "Receive the Lord's blessing. The Lord blesses you and watches over you. The Lord makes his face shine upon you and be gracious to you. The Lord looks kindly on you and gives you peace. In the Name of the Father, and of the Son, and of the Holy Spirit."

"Amen."

Time passed, and Mike stood alone in front of Maggie and David's graves. All the slots filled beside them, John would rest further down the graveyard. The glass bottle now empty in his hand, memories washed back of both hollow days when the granite stones before Mike were fresh. Twice he had committed to maintaining the sites with flowers and company, twice the pain made it far easier to stay away. How many years had it been?

A figure emerged from somewhere behind him; Mike sensed it far before he ever bothered to look. Eyes fixed but not taking in the words on the tablet, he noted that he swayed before the stones.

"How did you swing an invitation?" Mike slurred as Juliet approached. "They meant for the event to be an exclusive list."

"I said I wanted to come and apologise for the tone of the interview."

"And do you?"

"I am sorry for pressing you so hard."

Mike nodded. The incident in the room flooded back as a distant scar. All of that misery felt like a lifetime ago. New scabs, humiliation and bitterness boiled near the surface.

How many times in the last few weeks had they hauled him out of one of the local pubs? Punters all too keen to buy the father of John Fitzgerald a pint soon came to regret such a decision when he stumbled over tables, vomited on floors and flew into drunken rages.

"Are these your wife and son?" Juliet quizzed, the awkwardness obvious even to Mike.

Again he nodded, words only wasted.

"Tell me about them."

Mike's eyes rose to meet Juliet's. No trick or game hung in her expression.

"I met Maggie when she was sixteen, I was twenty. At the local she was one of my mates from down the pit's sister. A mischievous smile and banter that stood its ground against working men years older than herself. Nobody cared back then about legal drinking ages; she was part of the community and the community looked after itself. Always the same place, same people, but after some time we sat together often. A pair, a couple or whatever else you wanted to call it. From that day and for the next twenty years, she never left my side. Stability to my temper, mischief to my madness, and a hell of a good mum to those boys. I thought we'd grow old and die together. Cancer doesn't care about your plans."

Mike's eyes lingered onto the gravestone a second longer. "Loving wife, mother, and sister." Words replicated a hundred times across the gravestones. A life condensed down to a generic sentence. The same size hole and same shaped box awaited them all. Once Maggie had been laughter, opinions and witty retorts. Now she existed as a fragment in the heads of those she had touched in a shortened life.

"David. David, to this day, is the strongest man I ever knew," Mike said as the words caught in his throat. "I had the boy for sixteen years and never failed to marvel at his resilience. If he had joined the army, he would have led it. If he had become a boxer, he'd have a championship belt. Instead, he lost his mum and grew up with an incapable father. All that strength wasted on being the man I should have been. It would have been a privilege to see what he could be, and I wish I had been there more to help him."

"How did he pass?"

"Suicide," Mike confirmed. "John found him."

The silence that followed allowed Mike's thoughts to drift out of the moment. A light breeze in the trees, the emptiness and stillness of the surrounding graveyard. For a fraction of time, there was peace.

"I lost my mum when I was in my teenage years. She was the nicest, sweetest woman I've ever met, yet that didn't account for anything. She still died while people who have treated others like shit and are shitty people themselves continue to live merry lives. I've been in enough people's heads to know that karma doesn't exist. No matter who you are or how you live your life, when your time comes that's it, whether you're young or old, rich or poor, good or bad."

"I could have done better. Been a better father, a better husband, a better person. Maggie's death was out of my control, but I made those years miserable for her. If I hadn't pushed those boys so hard, maybe both would be alive now."

"You can't save everyone," Juliet said, a hand squeezing his shoulder. "Whether that be a family member, spouse, or friend. Sometimes the darkness within wins out. There's no amount of love, attention, affection, and support you can give that can save them from themselves. You could do everything in your power to help them and still fall short, because ultimately it's not your battle to fight."

"And yet I fell short," Mike turned with tears in his eyes. "I was a young man once. I could look into the mirror and see a person with a hundred different options staring back. You blink and nineteen has turned into twenty-nine. Blink again, and suddenly the man staring back isn't familiar at all. You've lost your youth. There's blood in your piss, you know exactly which knee is the bad one and someone has spent all your youth. Squandered it. All these fucking years have passed and I have no way of turning back the clock and fixing my mistakes. What's the point in it all if I'm already past the point where any decision I make matters?"

"I don't know what you want me to say," came Juliet's measured response. "There isn't a quote or a profound statement I can give you that will bring your family or the years back. All I can say is that my father has spent the last five years in a home, an empty shell of a person. Time keeps going by, whether or not you like it. At least you still have time to change some things. And the ability."

Dull rage clawed at Mike's insides as he stood before the gravestones a while longer. A light touch on his shoulder, a "sorry for your loss", and Juliet left. "The military record is fake," he called. Juliet stopped in his tracks and gazed at him.

"There was a letter. He went to Leeds and became a cleaner. I hope you can do something more with that than I can."

Juliet hovered somewhere behind Mike, but his back turned to her as he once again he watched alone. Eventually she left. Not a rotten man, a murderer or a rapist. Not a hated man, although disliked by many who would care to remember him.

There was nothing special about Mike. So why was he still there? Better men and women lay in graves all over. If their God had a plan, why bother with Mike?

Chapter Fifteen

Sirens blared as the impatient convoy tore through the streets of London. On pavements bystanders watched the cars speed past, curious as to the events of the day. In one of the vehicles sat Juliet in the back seat. Intelligence gathered showed that a homemade bomb for a terrorist attack was being manufactured on the premises. Akin to nothing more than a sniffer dog, Juliet was to walk the property listening out for any clues or phrases in the heads of those arrested.

The action had already taken place, much more brashly as an armed team and bomb disposal unit swept the premises. Agents had found evidence of bomb manufacturing and there was a pressure to reach anybody in a further-reaching terrorist community before word got out of the arrests. Already chatter in both the media and on social networks was spilling out concerning the raid.

By the time Juliet reached the place of residence, she walked past a blue police ribbon and a destroyed door. She followed a trail of destruction from the trashed lounge where two annoyed young men sat rabbiting at the officers involved, guns pointed at their handcuffed, seated bodies did little to disrupt the flair the two displayed. *Freedom, justice, patriotism* flew through their minds with conviction.

Months had passed since John Fitzgerald's murder, and though Juliet didn't want to acknowledge it, she had sensed a change in her role already. Gone were the murder cases that had so often filled her workload, a shift happening in attention towards more domestic-based threats.

John Fitzgerald's murder left Britain exposed. For years the government had cut police numbers, military equipment, and intelligence resources. Why were they needed when the country had an indestructible superhero? John's murder had opened the box for buried rage to emerge.

Domestically, Britain had pulled up the drawbridge, as had its European allies, officially until a time where safety could be guaranteed again. The deferring of the Schengen zone had led to protests in Ireland at implementing border checks on goods and at the Northern Irish border. This hard border was a breach of the Good Friday Agreement, but all over the world tensions had emerged.

In the US, police had used excessive force to combat their own domestic disturbances, and widespread violence had consumed cities as protesters railed against the police as an establishment. In the South Seas, China had become embroiled in territorial disputes with many of its neighbours, while in more than one Middle Eastern country there had been anti-government protests that turned violent. Pent-up rage that had never boiled to the surface no longer had an individual to suppress the outcome. Had John Fitzgerald ever involved himself in the inner workings of international politics? No, but the threat had always been there.

Taking a moment, Juliet allowed her eyes to do a quick sweep of the place. Stripped bare, the architect for the terraced house had likely envisaged a family home. The fireplace gutted and the carpets long since removed, the house was a lab rather than an actual residence. Mattresses on the floor, cupboards bare of food. This was no place of home comforts.

"Garret," Juliet said as she took a seat on the kitchen counter. The name had popped into both of the men's heads in the last minute, and she quickly scribbled down the name. Out of sight of any suspect in the property while they were 'processed', Juliet had free rein to dive into their head in an environment full of stimuli.

The officers themselves kept their distance, enough to monitor the cuffed suspects while allowing them to stew nervously on their knees. Name after name, first and second names came forth and Juliet quickly amassed a list of people and what appeared to be street names. Soon the full weight of the British intelligence service would knock on more doors, arresting more suspects and killing the roots of the terrorist weed.

Satisfied with the volume of information Juliet possessed on her list, officers led the two suspects to their waiting transportation, and Juliet too. There had been trouble in London again last night and the route taken was an odd one, a backstreet here and diverting around an obstacle there. In the boroughs where there had been rioting, the evidence of trouble from the night before was clear. The odd charcoal skeleton of a burnt-out car, some spray paint and blown litter into the gutters. Police and military vehicles outnumbered everybody, and the driver did well to avoid the blockades, assisted by bare streets that the public were sensibly staying away from.

Juliet's eyes swept over the urban streets. Snaking through the traffic, a car with a driver up top, the following days mapped out for her. Rioter after rioter, thug after thug, until the pool of current sin was drained. Then it would be onto the next one, maybe a rape or a murder followed by another and another. If Juliet was lucky, it would be a paedophile or a serial killer next. Anything to break the mould.

At a traffic light her eyes fell on a homeless man sat on a cardboard seat, sporting ripped and torn clothes with filthy hair and a rugged beard. The man said nothing to the few passers-by and for a second their eyes met, a sarcastic hand from the man the only noticeable connection as the car moved. She'd heard a story once, done little to verify the truth, that a charity had spent a tremendous amount of money on the local homeless population. Equipped with expensive sleeping bags and jackets for the winter, the charity secured fresh shaves and haircuts for all. Within weeks the clothes, sleeping bags and shoes were all found abandoned or missing, the homeless population back to their old, rugged looks. When questioned, each had a similar answer. The fancy clothes had made them look human, coping and okay, and the donations had dried up. So long as you were homeless and wanted a handout, the public expected you to stay and act poor.

The thought clung to Juliet as the car moved from one traffic light to the next. Case by case and day by day, she got another day older and a little closer to the end. A dark thought, death, yet an inevitable truth human beings put out of their mind as much as possible. Even John Fitzgerald had died, someone that seemed to have tricked the inevitable end to every lifespan. Despite a world in possession of people of extraordinary gifts and talent, the old sins remained. The homelessness, the poverty and the hunger. In what they labelled civilisation, the basic needs of food, shelter and warmth had not changed since humanity's creation, yet still proved an obstacle.

Then there had been the funeral. A letter that allegedly confirmed that John's military record was a simple fantasy. In the past days of the investigation, Juliet had any requests for access to the fellow soldiers rejected, told it was out of her remit. Yet the doubt had kept nagging at her. What they were hiding? They had arrested Casper, but there was more to it and she knew it.

Pressing events had pulled Juliet away from the case. That the streets of the UK would be just as safe without a superhero to police them was laughable, but Juliet understood the politics just fine. The public wanted a leader and a government to be in control, just enough to maintain order. That meant going hard and being relentless against those involved in the destruction.

The police created a hotline to take down reports, members of the public urged to call in any suspects. A patriotic tone of stiff British resolve and strength got the phones ringing off the hook. Looters, whether taking a television set or a bag of sweets, were easiest to catch. Police caught many because of the boasting of the crimes on social media, only for friends and followers to report the crimes. They were small-fry that the police and prosecutors had grand fun with, racking up the convictions and plea deals. If you plead guilty you get this deal, if you try to fight it, we will fuck you as hard as we can. Most got the message. The cases were running like clockwork on riot-related offences.

Juliet's function had become similarly robotic. One after another, those accused who were proving harder to pin down would sit down for an interview. Gang members, anarchists or just normal people where evidence of involvement was thin. Like a barcode scanner at a supermarket checkout, Juliet read the mind of the person for any word, phrase or feeling. One by one she relayed what she heard – objects, street names, places and names. The agents pressed on, slapping tables and puffing out chests to show how angry they were and how much they knew. A fair few buckled, fell for the bluff. The rest would take longer.

Quitting had been a constant in Juliet's mind long before the events of the last year. A world out there in need of help, infinite help. So much that Juliet felt she could spend a lifetime doing her role and not make a dent. Aged eighteen, grabbed from school and offered it all, money and opportunity all in exchange for use of her gift. For a long time now, she stumbled through the days in a blur. Not excited, not challenged. Juliet guessed that was why there was that sentiment to do one thing a day that scares you. Not because those things may be the right thing to do or will work out. It's because some people die at twenty-five and aren't buried until seventy-five.

Alone in her thoughts and, as much as Juliet would never say it, she knew there was no quitting. As the last British citizen with abilities, she was a valuable resource, too valuable to lose. The way the world was moving, Juliet felt ever so slightly a hostage to the situation, an invisible chain she dare not test the mettle of too intensely. Juliet had needed a focus outside of work. John Fitzgerald had been killed, murdered, yet Casper Smith was no lone wolf in it all. Something or someone far bigger had pulled the strings, switching his powers off to facilitate the murder. Juliet vowed that she would not rest until she had her *reason*.

That evening, Juliet considered the possibility she was mad. Before her, pinned up all across the walls, were newspaper clippings, printouts from blogs and websites and her own scrawls. John Fitzgerald's face was everywhere, pins and thread linking something of a timeline together. If anyone were to swing by, they would think the case obsessed her.

The truth was more extreme than that; she knew it had consumed her.

Chapter Sixteen

"Breaking news coming into us in the last few seconds, Casper Smith, the man accused of murdering John Fitzgerald, has been pronounced dead following an attack in prison this afternoon."

Shock no longer registered much with Mike Fitzgerald as he watched the news presenter rattle out the details of the story before his eyes. No warning from the police, or the government, Mike digested the breaking story in his mind along with everybody else. There it all was. The case over. John gone and any chance of justice had bled out in a prison shower.

Little had happened since the funeral that concerned his son. After they arrested Casper Smith, it quickly became clear, they had captured his son's killer. Headlines proclaiming they had caught the murderer rapidly replaced those referencing the chaos at the eulogy. An emergency call had reported what they thought was a body. Instead it was the overdosed but very much alive Casper. When police ran blood tests on the stains soaking his clothes, they discovered that the DNA profile was not his but John Fitzgerald's.

On the news and television, Casper's mother stood front and centre as the sole weeping defence for her son in the days to follow. A lonely presence as the public and press called for the death penalty under the loophole of treason, the one given as justification. Every day the media hounded her doorstep, protested outside Parliament and the prison.

From exclusions and expulsions at school to petty thefts and burglaries to fuel an escalating drug habit, Casper had for many years rejected a civilised society. One look at the man – skeletal in figure with fragmented teeth and a hollow stare – and you could not fight the urge to look away. Yet here was one woman, confronted every day with the venom and hatred, who refused to stop defending her son.

Was it a cover up? A conspiracy? Nobody would care now the murderer was dealt with. Mike switched the television off, an unwillingness to allow himself to be bombarded with footage of his son's killer. Unlike John's funeral, there would be nobody at Casper's. As Mike digested the headlines before him, he considered that, out there at least, there was one other parent more alone than he was.

Everyday Mike hauled himself from the sanctuary of sleep into the darkness of the day. Headaches raged, the blood in the toilet had become pools, and his grip on mind and body waned. The dreams of David and John in the maze had become relentless. No longer did he chase his two sons through the labyrinth. With chaos in their eyes, they screeched with inhumane noises, ferocious as they gave chase after their father. Mike would scuttle as fast as he could, the threat behind him always approaching. He would awake terrified, the alcohol the only thing able to put the terror back in the bottle for a few hours.

Routine had become a distant memory. One day Mike lingered in the doorway of David's old bedroom, cast his eyes over a room that had once breathed with life and potential. Lingered was the correct word, that's what Mike did – like a stale smell, he clung to the sides. Once that room had been all a little boy had to call home, all he had to come back to. Now not even the ghosts wasted their time in its four walls. Mike flicked to the clock and outside. The time read three in the morning; he'd risen only a couple of hours before.

David's bedroom had been the one where it had happened, where John had found his older brother hanging by a belt. When Mike finally stumbled home from the pub, steaming, the body had been taken down and taken away. A despondent son in the front room. Eyes raw, red, hatred in his eyes. Mike had buried that memory just as he had buried everything else.

The booze had lost its ability to numb. Ruthless in its consumption, Mike still couldn't keep the shakes, anxiety and terror at bay. A recluse in his home, distant from the pubs in town, Mike could only muster the courage to scamper to the corner shop and back. The windows blacked out with newspapers, Mike did all he could to blockade himself from the world beyond it. But the world didn't stop playing its games in his mind. All the haunting memories from over the years, all the horrors he'd seen and took part in. The drink couldn't rob him of it all.

One night, so late and dark there was barely a car on the road, Mike let his legs walk him the direction he wanted to go. On the bridge, above the railway track he looked down upon the metal that spread all the way into the distance. The east coast line, from London to York, through Newcastle and to Edinburgh. Every day the train sped past Bellington with not much more than a passing glance or concern. Nothing bothered to stop at Bellington much anymore. It was a place people went to die, or stayed to.

As Mike watched a late night train speed underneath him, shaking the foundations of the bridge, he considered whether destiny always had this in mind – God's punishment, robbing him of anybody he loved until he became the very last. Was this his punishment, suicide alone in the cancerous town he'd never been able to leave? Was that the end for men like Mike? Violent men meeting a violent end?

Half an hour passed as Mike swigged from a bottle of rum. As another train shot past at an astonishing speed, Mike's hand gripped the stone wall tighter. If he got the timing right, one big lift over the top and it'd all be over. Mike pictured his body cracking the front of the train, a traumatised driver braking with the damage already done.

There'd be those muttering darkly to themselves at the selfishness of the method, angered at the inconvenience. There'd also be the sympathetic, the passengers left hollowed out by it. An incident on the tracks was how they'd describe it, at least until the papers picked up who exactly Mike was.

The one Mike pitied most was the driver, the unwilling participant in his demise. Would they look after them? Offer the counselling to move past the horror Mike would rain down upon them? As Mike hovered at the bridge's brick, all the thoughts of his sons in his mind, he walked away. Too much of a coward to live, too much of a coward to kill himself either.

There was always a guy, everybody knew their own. Maybe the deadbeat from high school, the rough and ready former co-worker, or the man with the reputation in the pub's corner. The kind of man that either knew someone or could source it themselves. Anything. *Anything*. A woman for the night, a weapon or something hard to consume. Mike knew his, a man called Harry.

In the working-men's club was where Mike found him. Alone, pint in hand, nobody in the place daring to look sideways at the man. Scarred knuckles clenched the remnants of a pint, the number consumed, lost.

"I want some heroin," Mike stated as he propped himself on the stool opposite. "Heroin and somebody to guide me through it."

"You don't want heroin, Mike," was all that Harry said, not breaking his gaze from in front of him. "Now fuck off."

That was the code, wasn't it? Junkie etiquette, not to shoot up a newbie because they didn't want them to turn out the same way. Unless you asked more than once, which Mike did.

The next night Harry, for a few notes, scribbled down an address on a napkin.

"Ask for Rust," was all that Harry said, scrunching the bank notes into his jacket pocket. "Now fuck off."

The house wasn't far from Mike's terrace. The next day, in the afternoon when he mustered the courage, he knocked on the door and a figure with wild ginger hair answered. Mike asked if he was the man named Rust and only suspicious and delirious eyes looked back. Mike flashed some bank notes, and the door opened wider, creating a path inside. For money, the man would be anyone Mike wanted him to be. Mike wanted him to be a guide.

The bank notes snatched, Mike dropped his coat to the floor and made his way into the front room. Over on the sofa a younger man slumbered, comatose, sprawled over the arm of a chair. Mike opted for a seat on a torn armchair as the man he presumed to be Rust walked into the kitchen and came back with a roll of aluminium foil, a pair of scissors, and some kitchen roll.

Rust took a bag of heroin from his pocket and placed it on the glass table. It was tiny, the size of half a nail on his little finger. Mike watched as Rust unrolled the foil, tore off a piece about ten inches wide, and shaped it into a neat square. Every step methodical and well-practised, Mike watched as Rust efficiently scorched every inch of the foil with a lighter. First it went black, but he quickly wiped off the residue to leave a beautiful silver sheen. He tore off another piece of foil and rolled it into the shape of a straw.

Using the scissors, Rust opened the bag, and sprinkled the powder, light brown, into a long groove he had crafted on the foil. Using the same lighter, he heated the underside of the foil, directly beneath the heroin, and that's when the drug came alive. The dull brown powder transformed into a magnificent, golden brown puddle.

Rust placed the tray at an angle and, like lava rolling down a mountainside, it oozed down the groove of the foil, leaving white smoky fumes in its wake. The smell was pungent, similar to smoked fish, and it wafted through the air. Rust went first, signalling Mike to watch as he used the straw he'd made to hoover up the fumes, some of which clung to the foil. With barely a breath left, he took a pull on a cigarette, and held it in for as long as he could. Mike remained mesmerised by the ritual, already hooked on the drug's charms.

Rust tilted the tray and began caressing the lighter on the underside of the foil, the crystal that had formed returning to its liquefied state. Once again rolling down the groove like molten rock, Mike inhaled deeply, chasing the fumes that followed in its trail. With his last breath, he sucked on the cigarette; the filter collapsing under the strength of his grip. He held it in for as long as he could, then gasped with a breathless exhalation.

Within a minute, everything changed. Thoughts left the room. Anxiety left the room. Fear left the room. A softening of the muscles. A faint tilting of the head. Mike plunged into the armchair. Agitation, all the weight from the previous years – all of it left the room. Varying waves of warmth stirred around his body. It felt good. Everything felt very good. Mike didn't remember his body ever feeling so much sensation through it; he didn't remember being capable of feeling so much pleasure. Everything melted around him, every problem, ache and pain. Nothing else mattered.

As the hours passed, Mike continued with further hits. The technique that had mesmerised him earlier became part of his own skill set, albeit sloppier. With every inhalation Mike fell deeper into stillness, his fears and the agony in his own mind dissolved. There was no need to escape his own mind, to get away from himself. The new world Mike had begun creating for himself was an inner world of bliss, where he floated weightlessly without concern. The actual world, Mike could always get another hit. With every line, that actual world felt further away, the alternative world, the heroin world, the shelter to be sought out. Everything was safe there. Everything was quiet.

When Mike next awoke, no nightmares had consumed him. The world that greeted him was one of calm. With lazy eyes he scanned the room, saw only darkness through the gaps in the blind. Mike eyed the remnants of his day and smiled, dissolving back into his chair. As he laid back, an itch tingled across his body, mostly on his wrists. Gradually, deliberately,

Mike clawed his nails back and forth, up and down his wrists. For what felt like an hour, his scratching became one of the most gratifying experiences of his life.

Outside, the light had brightened and a flicker of it crept inside through the gaps. Usually the morning light brought only depression for Mike, the gloom and darkness of the night masking how he felt. But with his new protective blanket, the depression never came.

Bringing himself to his feet, all the money gone, Mike headed for the door, still light and free as if a cloud. The world outside, the real one he had returned to, lay in the twilight before morning broke. On his stagger home from Rust's house, Mike failed to encounter another human being, only the birds singing for company. Usually the sound of birds in the morning only brought a wave of depression and despair washing over Mike. Yet as Mike listened, he found only peace.

Once home, the nauseousness began. Mike dashed for his bathroom as sick moved up through his throat. An endless, dense mass, dropped into the sink below. The consistency was like baby food, full of lumps, and it wouldn't stop coming. A valve had been loosened, and the force of the vomit proved unrelenting. When it finally stopped, the remaining sick sat deep in the sink, the water from the tap unable to soften its dense nature. Mike swirled it around with his hand, attempting to force the water and vomit to mix, but it didn't work. As the watery sick drained down the sink, the stodgy lumps remained. Scooping them out, Mike hauled handful after handful into the toilet bowl before flushing it.

The moment should have shamed Mike, just as all the moments throwing up alcohol down the toilet that had come before did. But the euphoria, the heroin pumping through his body rejected any intrusion of negativity. There wasn't a care in the world that could burst Mike's bubble. Whatever pain he would go through, whatever ill thought entered his mind, the heroin would be close, the heroin would look after him.

Mike knew as he sat in his front room he would rob banks for the feeling, destroy lives to get the high again. Everything else would settle for less.

Chapter Seventeen

The government had faked John's military history; Mike had confirmed as much. Who could have the influence, scale and motivation to pursue such action?

The truth, as limited as it was, had become clearer to Juliet. John left home at sixteen, moved to Leeds and became a cleaner. At some point, the UK government recruited John into the shadows of the intelligence services. For a few years he had worked behind closed doors, and away from public eyes before his emergence at the Cherwell School fire. Obsessively re-watching the footage and press conference, there was no doubt in her mind this was no government request and a break from protocol. Why John had acted at this specific moment was unknown.

The questions still massively outweighed the answers in Juliet's possession. The heroin in John's body, the tattoo on his chest, scars on his body and ability to switch off his abilities. Who was Alice, the name he muttered drunk at the bar? Why was the military record faked? So many avenues for exploration remained unanswered. Patiently, Juliet had mapped out angles and possibilities for access.

The funeral for John Fitzgerald had been an empty casket, his body being kept in a static state as the government attempted to resurrect him or discover the key to his abilities. The information had been there, front and centre of the Prime Minister's mind. Even in death, John was still theirs. Mike had been there, a broken shell of a man. Tom's anger at the interview haunted her. In his spiral downwards he had found valuable information for her search, but at what cost? The man she had spoken to at the funeral had very few positive roads to head down.

The riskiest element of Juliet's investigation would be her next steps. With all that was going on politically, with the riots and the breakdown of international politics, there were risks she had to manoeuvre around. Juliet was too high-profile and well known. If the government or media discovered that she was investigating the murder still, or that there was maybe some kind of cover-up to John's death, there would be fallout. Everybody knew what had happened to Casper Smith, and even she had doubts whether it was a legitimate murder by a prisoner. The possibility it was Juliet's own government never left her mind. They had lied about the military record and the empty casket. What else were they hiding and what would they do to keep it hidden?

Day-to-day, Juliet continued with what they used her to do, one eye always glancing over the shoulder. The night was her domain.

Distracted one day, Juliet spent her time between cases and interviews flicking through celebrity columns and articles to trace any recent activity of Candice Crawford. During the eulogy she had been the only individual she had witnessed with any realistic first-hand knowledge of John Fitzgerald. This information was hers alone. It had never been reported up the ladder with the killer caught so soon after. Yet the publicly known mind-reader, and the publicly known celebrity, coming into contact for no reason? Just more obstacles to skirt past.

The paparazzi photos of Candice leaving coffee shops, going food shopping and bikini pictures abroad with the odd romantic linkage, were as deep as the articles dared to go. Candice sure enough had done stints in rehab before she and John were allegedly even an item. The likelihood of her knowing who John had sourced drugs from was likely. They had found John's body in London; the possibility remained high he had gained and taken the drugs had in the same city, Candice's home turf.

In an official capacity, Juliet had no business contacting Candice. Her involvement in the investigation had been closed off with the arrest, and subsequent murder, of Casper Smith. Yet Juliet continued to use the intelligence she had access to, to reveal an address in Kensington where Candice lived. There was a coffee shop nearby where Candice would have regular morning breakfast meetings with her personal assistant – her Instagram posts revealed as much.

Over weeks Juliet made herself a regular face and on personal terms with Gino, the man who owned the coffee shop. A morning coffee was now a staple of her routine to dismiss suspicion. The car regularly came to pick up her in the morning from here after her personal training session. To all those who cared to listen, Juliet raved about her new personal trainer and coffee shop, and they could ask no questions concerning her presence there. It was all one big coincidence.

Common ground was not a hard thing to find when she had full access to Gino's thoughts. Originally from Madeira, he had moved over in the nineties and started his own coffee shop. An avid football fan, he primarily followed Real Madrid as Cristiano Ronaldo came from his slice of the island. His only daughter was studying in Bristol. Familiar with neither Madeira, Real Madrid nor the University of Bristol, Juliet ensured she quickly became well-versed in all three. The payoff was enthusiastic conversations with the owner and no issue getting a table in a well-known and exclusive haunt of the rich and famous. The rest would be a matter of patience.

Instagram had kept Juliet up to date with the comings and goings of Candice. L.A., a fashion show in Milan and a quick rest in Bora Bora had been the story of the past few weeks. Her team had taken the most high-definition shots and uploaded them every step of the way. Juliet was ready and waiting the day that Candice made her return to Gino's coffee shop for avocado and salmon on sesame seed toast. A photo of the meal snapped for social media too, obviously. Yet neither this venture, the second nor third, was where Juliet made her move. Likely having one shot at the situation, the risk was too large and so patience was key.

Finally, the day came.

Glamorous, cool and sophisticated was the game of Candice Crawford. Thirty, dressed in clothes that hung off her body like it was destiny for them to be paired together. There wasn't a hair out of place, or a blemish on her costume. Into the coffee shop she strode, designer handbag in one hand and mobile in another. Costume was the description Juliet chose because everything was manufactured, rehearsed and designed with an end goal in mind. Before their 'meeting', she'd Googled and scrolled through a thousand images. Even on the 'casual' days with baggy clothes and unkempt hair, the look was still well-practised.

Juliet left Candice to relax, have her breakfast and order two oat-milk lattes for herself and her assistant. After a few weeks away from London, there were plans to make and business to attend to. Juliet's opportunity came when the assistant went to the bathroom. As soon as she did, Juliet was on her feet and, casually as she could, was at Candice's table.

"Think of a number between one and a thousand," Juliet stated as she dropped herself into the seat opposite. There was one shot at this. Staff were tight on custom to the coffee shop and wary of either fans, paparazzi, or stalkers infiltrating the walls.

Momentarily surprised, Juliet sensed the instinct within Candice to seek help, whether from her personal assistant or one of the staff. On her phone her eyes flicked up and widened, but before the situation could escalate, Juliet tried to dilute the fear. "Humour me," she said. "Just think of a number, in your head."

Before Candice could really register what was happening, Juliet spoke again. "Four hundred and sixty-two. Now go again."

Candice's brow curled in confusion. There was a crazy woman opposite her. The coffee hadn't woken her up enough for such an interaction.

"Seventy-six," Juliet said calmly. "I'm like John Fitzgerald, except I can read minds. Think of as many numbers as you need to, and I can give them to you straight back. I'm here because I need to talk to you."

Wary but no longer terrified of being shot or stabbed, Candice lay her phone down but remained on edge enough to leap to her feet if she needed to. "I've already spoken to the police months ago."

"I know," Juliet replied as she flashed Gino a smile. He had noticed her abandoned empty table with the coat hanging over the back of the chair. "I was at the eulogy and you proved to be the only person I encountered who knew John Fitzgerald, properly I mean, rather than on a surface level."

"But they got the killer. I don't really know what I can offer or what you need from me?"

"I'm not here on official business," Juliet assured her. "Truthfully, they have pared back the investigation, but I'm sure you know that John's murder goes further than Casper Smith. I want five minutes, to know the guy I'm investigating."

At this point Juliet caught the eye of the personal assistant hurriedly heading back to her seat. Gone for less than five minutes, a crazed fan was already harassing her boss.

"Excuse me, but Candice is on a tight schedule today and–"

"It's okay Hilary," Candice reassured over with a smile. "I'll be five minutes, I'm just having a chat with an acquaintance. Steal her chair and I'll call you over once we're done."

Scanning the face of her employer, Hilary took a seat at the empty table but kept a close eye for a minute on the vibe of the conversation, checking for any danger.

"Five minutes," Candice declared. "What would you like to know?"

"Can you describe how you met and what the relationship was like?" Juliet began as she nodded to the assistant who was observing proceedings.

Playing with one of the many rings on her fingers, Candice began. "We met at a party, one of those functions designed for celebrities to network. He looked a little bored, and we shared a cigarette. It's fair to say we hit it off and we'd hang out when we could. It was romantic for a time, but destiny dictated something like that would never last."

The words were full of lies, but Juliet rejected confrontation. It would be better to keep Candice onside and see where she would slip up. "What was he like as a person?" Juliet pressed.

Lost, yet the words that left Candice's lips painted a different picture. "Happy that he was doing well in the world. He loved what he did, the fruits of his labour giving a meaning to his life so many of us crave. He's a tragic loss, not just in my life but a billion others."

"And do you know who'd want to end such a life, who'd even have the knowledge how?"

Candice shook her head. "I probably have the same level of knowledge you do. He never really kept anybody that close."

A tender pause hung in the air after that, and Juliet picked her time to play her card. In a hushed whisper she recanted information that would get her in very serious trouble. "They found John's body with heroin in his system. I understand you have had stints in rehab, so the obvious question I want to ask is if you and John ever... shared any experiences like that?"

The tension had risen and Juliet prayed she had been delicate enough in her approach. Softly as she could Juliet finished, "This is part of no official investigation and is completely off the record. I'm genuinely just after a direction. If he had drugs in his system the day he died, I need to know where they came from and who he likely had them with."

"John and I would usually do drugs when we hung out. Nothing hard though, only cannabis. At parties, cocaine was usually being passed around like candy – I suppose he likely had some then. Heroin and anything else? I can't confirm, but it's sad if he hit that point."

Candice remained silent but pensive for a moment. Her

thoughts were a blur, never settling. As Juliet listened to Candice, she knew the facts would not be entirely accurate. Memories had blurred and morphed in her mind to only an interpretation of what happened. But the feelings attached, the emotional connection and hidden skeletons remained. Those were the clues and indications Juliet was after and hoped would give her a sense of the version of John Fitzgerald that really existed.

"We met in the circumstances I said," Candice confided. "The thing the public doesn't see about the celebrity events is how manufactured they all are. We spend half of award ceremonies with agents and PR people, speaking with other celebrity PR teams. It's a business, networking and making deals while the cameras pan around the empty seats. There's never any fun to it, it's all for show, our brands. One particular night I could barely stand it and slipped out a fire exit for a cigarette where I found John and we shared a couple. He was as bored as I was, no idea who I was, but we shared jokes about the state of these events and came to a mutual understanding. I joked that my team were trying to find bachelors to pair me with and John offered to hang out again sometime."

"So they organise the celebrity relationships?" Juliet reacted.

"Some," Candice admitted. "It's good for all parties to manufacture these fake relationships. It's all about being spotted by the paparazzi at the fashionable bars, restaurants and parties. The more the magazines and gossip talk about you, the more attention and work you naturally receive. It delighted my team that somehow I'd swung a date with THE John Fitzgerald. It wasn't like that though, even though the magazines painted that way. We hung out, smoked weed, talked and spent our time mocking it all, 'real life' behind the scenes."

"The heroin," Juliet emphasised. "Is there anybody who might point us toward who the most recent batch of drugs came from?"

"I'm afraid not," Candice replied with certainty. "If it was in London, I could tell you, but I don't know Northumberland at all."

"Northumberland?" Juliet questioned. As soon as she did, Candice shared a nervous look with her assistant.

"I'm sorry for interrupting your breakfast and jumping on you like this," Juliet lamented as she found Candice looking increasingly uncomfortable. "I'm grateful for your time and will leave you be. But you mentioned Northumberland. I know that's where he was from, where his father lives. What's the connection?"

"We went there once," Candice acknowledged. "Just once. He had a place in London but there was a place that was just his, unofficial, and he kept it very much a secret. I wasn't meant to know where we were going but, well, I was curious. When we were out there, I looked at the map on my phone. A place called Rothbury, but just outside of that."

"Thank you," Juliet said as she mulled over it all. At every turn there was a wall in front of John. A distant father, closed off to relationships and a dependence on drugs. A man keeping his cards close to his chest. "Is there anything more about John, even the slightest idea of the man I'm investigating, that you'd like to share?"

"He was still human beneath the armour," Candice stated as she fiddled with the ring on her finger. *Drunk one night, John had used it for a fake proposal. They had laughed themselves to tears over the prospect of selling the photos to magazines.* "On that

TV footage they keep showing, he looks unstoppable. Behind closed doors he was as insecure at the rest of us."

The conversation finished, Juliet thanked Candice for her time. Something had been clear, away from the words and behind the scenes of the conversation. When Candice spoke of relationships, Northumberland and touched the fake ring on her finger, a solo word stayed at the forefront of her mind. The word held no malice, no anger or hatred in Candice's mind. Yet beneath the flickering memories of their platonic relationship the word held power, association and Juliet didn't quite know what to do with it. Candice and John had never been lovers, never entangled in anything more than a brief friendship.

What Juliet learnt from inside Candice's head was that John Fitzgerald was gay.

Chapter Eighteen

Autumn had gripped the country as Juliet hurried down empty streets. For another year beer gardens had emptied, jumpers dug out of wardrobes and even the bravest cyclists spent some commutes on the bus or Tube. Night was setting in, a chill and rain in the air, as Juliet periodically pulled a phone out of her pocket to follow directions. The estates she scampered through felt safe enough, wide and well-lit, but she could never be too sure. She'd heard enough of the ugly thoughts of passers-by before.

The terraced house Juliet marched up to blended perfectly alongside its neighbours. A steep staircase leading to a large doorway. On the phone Leo had confirmed he lived in a house share, a lot on the street were, but he'd have privacy. Leo had been the man who had approached Juliet on the day of the murder and who had revealed that John had been missing for nearly two weeks from the public eye. The website he'd helped moderate, Fitzgerald Watch, now lay defunct and unused. Juliet had given Leo her business card, not the other way around. On the website, she messaged for him to call the mind-reader. Leo had broken the basic code, and they set the meeting.

A loud knock on the door and Juliet waited, moments passing before a young male in gym gear answered the door.

"I'm here to see Leo." Juliet smiled. "Is he there?"

The housemate looked at Juliet with a hint of surprise. Guests were rare for Leo, especially female ones.

"He'll have his headphones in, it's up the stairs and on your left."

Juliet entered the property and climbed up the stairs. To her right was the bathroom, the door open, and a radio played down in the basement, presumably where the kitchen was. Once again Juliet knocked on the door frame and this time Leo answered, slightly bewildered as his eyes fell on Juliet.

"It's seven," he stated rather than asked.

"It's seven," Juliet confirmed with a smile.

Suddenly Leo was in a rush. "I logged on at five, I thought I had ages," Leo flustered. Not even knowing where to begin, the figure before Juliet was almost comic as he froze in horror at the state of his room. Instant noodle pots and energy drinks lined the windowsill of a room that possessed the distinct smell of takeaways. A significant laundry pile filled the corner. His duvet lacked covers and without showing her slight revulsion, Juliet took a seat at the end.

The pride and joy of the room was a desktop computer, three screens with a neon trim. Juliet knew little about computers, she mostly stuck to her phone, but the computer looked like one Leo had built himself. There was even an elaborate gaming chair for use with it.

The wall of Leo's room looked much like Juliet's. Newspaper cut-outs of many John Fitzgerald news stories lined the walls. Yet dozens seemed unrelated. Leo had plastered alternative stories about business acquisitions and middle-page stories alongside. Most of the business stories concerned weapon purchases, which countries were investing, and from whom.

"You and John never crossed paths much," Leo stated, noticing that Juliet was admiring his wall. "Why do you think that was?"

"If you'd asked me six months ago, I'd have told you it was because how busy we were both kept. An ability doesn't allow for much of a private life. Plus, he was the golden boy, I was always the footnote in any article."

"And if I asked you now?"

"I think he didn't want me in his head, close enough to read his thoughts," Juliet acknowledged.

"I bet you hear all kinds of gossip," Leo responded eagerly.

"You'd think so," Juliet replied. "But what's gossip if you don't know the people involved? Workplace drama, spousal arguments or anxiety at home are ninety percent of what occupies the mind."

The answer seemed to burst Leo's bubble somewhat, and he turned his back to Juliet as he became immersed in his triple-screen set up.

"All very safe," he commentated aloud. "I have used the Tor browser."

"Is that a VPN?"

"With VPNs there can still be data leaks, where encrypted data gets transmitted. That includes IP leaks, and DNS leaks. The Tor browser, or the onion router, sends my data through several anonymous servers. In doing so, it becomes considerably more difficult to identify what I'm doing online. It originally came out of research done for use by US intelligence. They had an obvious need for secure online communications."

"I'll take your word for it," Juliet laughed, the language alien to her. "But thank you. As I said on the phone, keeping this search secure is crucial."

"So what is it you've found?" Leo enquired eagerly.

"I heard from a reliable source that John had a house in a place called Rothbury, Northumberland."

"Interesting," Leo mulled aloud. "We always knew the flat in London was nonsense, but Rothbury never came up. As far as we ever heard, he never returned to the North East. Have you learnt anything else?"

Leo had his uses. But he also struck Juliet as the person who'd be prone to blab any gossip he heard right onto his message boards. It was a risk, Juliet being there, but a calculated one.

As Juliet waited on the edge of Leo's bed her eyes drifted to a recent newspaper cutting on the wall. The face of Marco accompanied the story, one that had captivated recent column inches.

Juliet never knew Marco Rossi well. His employment with British intelligence put him more on the John Fitzgerald side of things than any of Juliet's investigations. Reputation-wise, she knew enough. Hard, efficient and uncharismatic, he was a soldier with his ability to manipulate fire as an extension of his skills. Alongside John Fitzgerald, his work and missions saved many lives.

Juliet's last encounter with Marco ended without an exchange of words. A solid stare and a fixed lack of emotion, Marco showed no warmth or recognition towards Juliet as she entered the room. Present for photos, scripted statements and interviews, the whole event only a public relations exercise.

Marco's appetite for violence had hit the headlines in recent days, but at the time only a rumour. They sealed details of his missions. There were only ever tales and rumours. Juliet heard stories of brutality, excessive burns to criminals, and a flagrant disregard for the damage his powers could cause. Officially, publicly or any substantial proof? Not a murmur.

Earlier that week Marco had died in an altercation in his home of Bologna. News stories revealed a dozen police call-outs for domestic abuse, battery, assaults and beatings with the same pattern. A neighbour or his fiancée would call; they'd throw him in the drunk-tank and then wouldn't press charges. Fights, brawls and altercations were common misdemeanours the authorities turned a blind eye to. Marco worked in a culture of violence, his private life showing that same nature too.

Two weeks after the last call, an argument had broken out in a bar, witnesses describing Marco as the instigator as a fellow patron of the bar bumped into him. A war of words ensued. A fight spilled outside. Marco burnt the opponent, but a punch levelled him and his head hit the curb. By the time paramedic arrived Marco had died, a daughter and fiancée left behind.

The case involved no major use of powers, but something had brewed in the media. The riots, foreign policy debates dominated headlines, a death penalty referendum discussed, and a Prime Minister looking weak in a time of crisis. But questions were beginning to be asked. *What happens if the next person with powers isn't like John Fitzgerald? What happens if they're a villain?*

Momentarily Juliet's mind flicked back to early in the investigation, the story from the barmaid in John's block of flats. Alone, drunk and muttering nonsensical words. Was John really who the world thought he was? Then there was the name, the damned name he'd been thinking about. "Does the name Alice ring any bells?" Juliet quizzed, praying for help out of the dead-end.

"Doesn't ring a bell, context might help?"

"Unfortunately, I have nothing more on the name. He just said it not long before he died in a moment of distress."

"Shame," Leo said as he turned and began typing. "I'll look into the Rothbury lead."

From Juliet's position on the edge of the bed, she couldn't really see what Leo was doing on his screen. All she could describe was a rapid pace, clicking, typing and pulling up various windows at an impressive speed. The longer he spent, the more he grunted and showed signs of discontent. In his mind, an internal monologue had begun. What he was seeing was odd, and he looped in other people in his network.

Apprehensive to interrupt Leo while he was in full-flow, Juliet listened to his thoughts. Using electoral registers, the land registry, satellite images and online maps, he'd mapped the town. Yet when he overlaid historic images, something strange occurred. Several local Northumberland maps from over the decades varied from what was now showing online, and Leo set to work carving out the difference between the versions. His attention focused on any gatherings of buildings or lanes that vanished. The process time-consuming, thorough, and arduous, a series of places appeared to vanish from existence in the recent decades.

"Here," Leo stated finally, with conviction. "If John had a house in Rothbury, it's right here."

"You're certain?" Juliet remarked, shocked. "Can you talk me through it?"

Leo pointed and clicked through a series of maps, building a complex picture. A road, clear on maps in the eighties, had disappeared. Previously a house lay nearby, but now only showed as a farmer's field. The sketches showed a drainage system underneath where the house had previously sat. On street view, the only roads that weren't covered were those that would have a potential view of the property, and zooming in too close from the satellite image was also banned.

"On and on I can go," Leo stated. "But that house right there... That is a house that somebody has tried very hard to bury."

Rothbury remained infamous in modern times for a 2010 police manhunt. Raoul Moat shot an ex-girlfriend, killed her new boyfriend, and blinded a police officer. A lockdown and siege of the rural community followed, with ex-footballer Gazza rocked up in a dressing gown with a finishing rod, beers and chicken to try and defuse the situation. Police declined the offer, and the situation ended in a standoff and Moat's suicide.

Every major news event across the last decade involved John Fitzgerald. Murders, manhunts, terror attacks involved a personal involvement. Yet as Juliet examined Rothbury, its recent history and read about the Raoul Moat manhunt, John Fitzgerald's name remained absent. A multi-day search, and no reasonable explanation online for his absence. The only explanation that made sense was that a headline had come to John's front doorstep, and he was forced to stay away. Rothbury proved to be a perfect missing piece in the jigsaw puzzle.

Rothbury was home to a population of two thousand people, its distance from London making it challenging to reach. Online became Juliet's only real avenue. Doing so without alerting suspicion proved even more difficult.

Juliet bought her train tickets at the station the next day up to the Rothbury, and booked a local pub with rooms. Everything was last minute, minimising the time any intelligence agency could track her movements or contain any breakthrough in the case. The riot situation having calmed, the leave of absence for a long weekend did not appear unusual and received approval with no fuss. The journey began with a four-hour train ride to a town called Morpeth, a nerve-wracking experience where Juliet never settled. At each stop Juliet pictured agents or police jumping aboard and arresting her. But stop after stop, with a ducked head and averted eyes, no such event occurred.

The train forced Juliet into the company of hundreds of members of the public. Gone were private helicopters and chauffeur-driven cars and in their place noisy thoughts, feelings and anxieties. The crying kids proved the worst. Even their own thoughts made little sense to them, and they wore their emotions permanently at the forefront. Her headphones blaring loud music, Juliet drowned out the voices as much as possible. During her busy journey, Juliet's heart never stopped beating a mile a minute.

Morpeth Station soon emptied as dozens both exited and boarded the train. No coffee shop, no waiting area, only a car park waited before Juliet. Renting a car required identification, a paper trail, and electronic transactions. A bundle of cash in her purse, withdrawn gradually over the previous weeks, Juliet rang a local taxi firm and made the final forty-minute part of the journey to Rothbury by car.

The driver found the pub in the centre, rooms plentiful in the off-peak season. Older couples appeared to be the main demographic, staying there, walking boots and warm clothing covering radiators and neatly paired together in the hallways.

The receptionist seemed accepting enough of Juliet's story that her family had moved in nearby and lacked a spare room. Excuse laid and money paid. The room on the second floor became hers for the long weekend.

Exhausted from the journey, Juliet held back from an immediate start to her search. Ditching her light overnight bag, she headed out into the town itself for a coffee and some food, finding a place that fit the bill. The soup of the day was homemade mushroom, the walls and lighting were bright, modern yet cosy all the same. Lining the walls were images of the Northumberland countryside. Miles upon miles of lush green hills, the town felt like another world away from the hustle and bustle of London.

Later, after a pint in a pub that evening, with no sense she was being watched, Juliet planned to walk the few miles between all the properties early the next day. Sipping the last of her beer, Juliet left a tip for the barman and departed for her room. The bar was deserted, excluding two local men deep in a discussion. They'd spied her from across the way, but seemed too involved in a discussion regarding local gossip.

Coming along the corridor, Juliet sensed somebody inside her room before she opened the door, her hand on the handle hesitating. The person inside was working, writing emails and considering phrasing. Debating what to do, Juliet spied the two men from the bar coming from either direction down the corridor. Like a poor scene in a movie, Juliet knew there was little she could do to evade the strangers, but she remained undisturbed. There was only one organisation that was interested in her and it was her employer.

As Juliet entered the room, a middle-aged woman sat waiting patiently on the chair working. Her blonde hair in a bob, in her forties and with a permanent, suspicious frown plastered across her face, Helen Becton was technically her boss. Juliet held the door for the approaching men who had followed her there. When everyone was inside, and without turning away from her laptop, Helen started to speak.

"Your credit cards belong to us, and even though you paid by cash, we saw the withdrawal near the station. That tripped a signal that you were on the move." Her voice came with no hint of ego, as if the thinking were so elementary it would be nothing to be proud of. "Your phone has its own inbuilt software to pick up phrases and searches. Even a VPN, proxies or other masking processes aren't fool-proof. Rothbury, John Fitzgerald. The first two searches alone gave the game away. That's not even including the reality that we've watched Leo intently since the murder from a distance. One of our work experience interns could have found you."

Juliet stood humbled by an individual that wouldn't even look her in the eye. Helen Becton was arguably the most powerful unelected figure in British politics. She was making notes on a parliamentary white paper, while just this morning had been speaking on the telephone with the Prime Minister. Juliet somewhat marvelled at the ease she was picking thoughts out from her head, but it was almost too easy, deliberate.

"Do you speak?" Helen asked as she put the laptop to one side and started speed-reading and highlighting papers. "All this noise you've been making, yet here you stand silent."

"We've met a few times before," Juliet said. "You know I speak."

Without skipping a beat, Helen replied, "You're in a room with the individual who has been tracking you. In a room with the person who has been your boss your entire career.

A person with a wealth of answers to everything you've been seeking, and you aren't asking questions?"

The woman flustered Juliet. Frosty in her speech, body language and mind, she saw Juliet as a mere crumb on the cake of everything she sought. So why bother at all?

"Ask a question," came a somewhat irritated request.

"Why are you here?"

"We gave you direct instructions to drop the case, yet you did not do so. I am here to make you stop being an irritation and tie up the loose ends. Speaking to your former partner Tom, you are unlikely to go down without a fight so I thought it best to come personally."

Juliet looked to the two men in the room, both relaxed in their stance and thoughts. Neither struck Juliet as hired hitmen and if she was to be mean, they looked more like men responsible for the paperwork than anything more physical.

"I want to find out the truth about John Fitzgerald," Juliet said as she tried to control the situation.

"Well, I gathered that sweetheart," Helen said as she finally peered up. "You are in the arse-end of nowhere. What I want to know is why?"

Juliet again found herself at a loss for words. To find the truth was the answer she wanted to give, but was it enough?

"I've dug into you. There's nothing personal tying you to the case and from a morality point of view, you don't seem to want to tarnish John's reputation. I want to know what it will take to make you go home and stay there. What is your motivation?"

"Curiosity," was the only word Juliet could muster. "I have nobody to tell, nothing to gain by knowing and no personal vendetta. I want a resolution from all of this."

"So ask away," was Helen's simple response as she put her phone down. Meanwhile, she waved the men away. "Signal's terrible anyway."

"Just like that?" Juliet replied, stumped by the forthright nature of the response. When Helen gave no response, Juliet had no choice but to ask.

"What happened to John after he left Bellington? Why hide the fact he was gay?"

"That's a sensible place to start," Helen answered. "John moved to Leeds and became a cleaner for a time, and around that period he started sleeping around, eventually concluding he was gay. Life fell apart a little after that – he moved between shitty jobs, and took harder and harder drugs. He hit our radar when he escaped a pair of handcuffs, phased right through them. The CCTV picked it up, and we closed that avenue down as quickly as we could. It was only a possession charge, and we made it go away. John worked for us."

"So why lie about a military record? Why bother with such a story?" Juliet retorted.

"Well, Cherwell had us chasing ourselves quickly," Helen admitted. "We never planned for any of you to go public, and then John was in the wrong place at the wrong time. I was furious he intervened. But he did, and we had to react. When announcing to the public that there was a man with superpowers who could, and had, taken down an entire army without a single casualty, putting them at ease is a priority. As you will see in the news at the moment, people do not trust abilities, they consider them dangerous. They certainly wouldn't have trusted them in the hands of a working-class boy from the North East. John came from a broken home, held no qualifications, and had a minimum wage employment history. Need I go on? The world, even now, is not ready for a homosexual superhero. Imagine the situation abroad with John in third-world nations, harbouring far more conservative opinions. There are countries John was being sent to that would execute men of his sexuality. We created a backstory that allowed John to continue his excellent work without terrifying Middle England. A straight, ex-soldier nobody needed to fear."

"And he was okay with all that?"

"Coming out as the world's first superhero presented enough anxieties. John had no wish to come out a second time. The deal we made let John live his life privately, however he wished, and we covered up as and when it was needed. The heroin was part of that. Rehab, therapy and all manner of treatments did not sort out the fact the man was a broken individual, so we left him to it. The one thing that kept him sane and happy was saving lives. If he shoved a needle in his arm or took men to bed, it didn't stop either side from getting what they wanted."

"What about the other cover-ups?" Juliet quizzed, still in awe she was getting all the answers on a plate. "The tattoo, the scars on his body, and how on earth his ability could have been switched-off."

"Quite a list," Helen remarked. "The tattoo marked the date of his wedding anniversary; his husband is in name only, a reminder of where he'd come from. No ring allowed, after all! From all the science we've been able to pull together, abilities manifest in individuals undergoing intense trauma. A suicide attempt in a bathtub was sufficient for John. Rather than a dozen abilities, it was the ability of matter manipulation. At a molecular level, John could alter his form to suit his needs, enhancing his physical abilities to whatever he desired. Part of this was regeneration and immortality, but rather than being a permanent feature, it was something he could switch off himself alone if he so chose. Hence the tattoo, the scars and the hiding of this truth."

Juliet stood in dumbfounded silence as she tried to absorb all the information.

"Let me get to the point and do the thinking for you," Helen suggested. "John died because he switched off his ability and, despite months of investigating, we do not understand how or why he would do so. No conspiracy. The whole situation took us by surprise as much as it did the rest of the world. Casper Smith, to our knowledge, was a tripped-out drug addict in the wrong place at the wrong time, and our current line of thinking is he murdered John. I need to know why."

"So let me get this straight, you think this whole thing was some kind of suicide attempt?" Juliet spat in confusion. It made little sense; yet Helen's thoughts were clear.

"I have had many months in the same boat as you, and I cannot come up with any reason either. If John wanted to die, I do not understand why he wouldn't just kill himself. Why allow it in such a brutal manner? I am at a loss for motivation."

"Why are you telling me this?"

"Because you are curious and have nobody to tell. Even if you did, there's no evidence and not a soul would believe you. Go to the papers or the media and they'd either laugh at you or ignore you. We are bulletproof, Juliet. The only reason you got close was because you had an inside track. The public out there? Why would they question it or really care with everything else going on? They're apathetic and their attention has moved on," Helen summarised.

"But equally, like you, I gather knowledge. My motivation is different to yours; I see information as a resource and like to fill my head with it. Knowing why John died is redundant at this point. Yet I still want to know. I have an ulterior motive for you, if you care to take it?"

Juliet didn't know what to say, her mind a blur. Months' worth of work had come to fruition before her eyes. They had answered all the hours of conspiracy theories, questions and dead ends in a single conversation. What terrified Juliet was that it all made sense. Since the murder, the world felt like it was drifting in a direction of fear. Would the British public have accepted someone with such baggage being so powerful?

"What do you want from me?" Juliet finally asked.

"There is another British citizen with abilities," Helen confided. "A girl by the name of Alice, eleven years old. She first came onto the radar at a young age, drawing some of the most disturbed drawings the local authority had seen from a child. They suspected sexual abuse. Our intelligence service got hold of the situation when those pictures she was drawing proved to be correct forecasts. The little girl could dream and draw the future."

"Alice," Juliet acknowledged, a sly smile appearing on her face. Not a red herring. "And you want me to get inside her head?"

"Indeed," Helen confirmed. "Towards the last months of his life, John took Alice into his confidence. We believe he was trying to mimic her ability, predict future events so he could be able to stop them. Any questioning meets refusal. We have no way to force the answers from her, she's in an institute and as an eleven-year-old child has protections in place. Those conversations may hold the key for why John shut off his abilities and allowed himself to die. I want you to find out the truth."

"And the catch?"

"She will already have likely dreamt you are coming, and it is likely to be the most challenging conversation you have had in your career," Helen stated. "Alice is… unlike anyone I have ever met. I questioned her personally, but it was no use. Hyper-intelligent, manipulative and the ability she possesses is one that has twisted a poor child up inside and created something else entirely."

"I'll do it, but you already knew that," Juliet replied. "But I have a last request, at least so this trip hasn't been completely wasted."

"You're hardly able to bargain," Helen lamented. "But go on, make the request."

"I'd like you to reach out to the husband and convince him to meet Mike."

"Why?"

"Because I stole from him any idea that John turned out okay," Juliet admitted. "A husband who loved him would have more of an impact than you know."

The world would remember John as a soldier, an aspirational hero with higher praise than saints and royalty. However, the near-religious entity was anything but. A brother, a son, a cleaner, a drug addict and, with his own baggage, a blend of a person masked from the wider world.

"I'll have a word with him." With that Helen folded up her laptop, stacked her papers and put them into her bag. "We'll be in touch with a date or time. Keep yourself free."

Chapter Nineteen

"You'll never have a high as perfect as your first," the voice in Mike's head taunted as he stumbled home. "But feel free to die trying."

For weeks Mike had been going to Rust's house, graduating to needles to minimise as much time he spent in the actual world as possible. The money had run out, and he'd pawned whatever he could. The withdrawal felt like the most intense flu he'd ever had, a scraping inside of his body and brain. Mike would do anything to keep it at bay. Rust's house had become more of a home than the one he returned to.

The euphoria still coursing through his veins from the night before, Mike could describe his sensation as one of cosiness. As he approached his house, a car too flash for his neighbourhood waited outside. An estate, black and well-waxed. Against it lent a man, muscular with well-groomed black hair. Hands clasped before him, the man eyeballed Mike from some distance away, stare unflinching as he approached.

"Mike Fitzgerald?" he said, his accent posh and from somewhere further south than Mike would know.

"That's the one."

"I'm John's husband. My name's Nick."

Mike felt his heart drop into his stomach, the statement like a punch to the gut. A hand outstretched on instinct, Mike shook it, the grip and shake firm. As he pulled the hand away, Mike tried to digest the statement but failed.

Mike's eyes immediately flicked to the man's left hand, a plain metallic band on the correct finger. As Mike's eyes flicked back up, a pair of hazel eyes behind a pair of horn-rimmed glasses gazed back. The man before him appeared normal enough. Not a crazed fan or oddball. Taller than Mike, at a guess around six foot, Nick resembled any normal bloke. Around thirty, he was dressed smartly in a navy jumper and blue denim jeans.

"He had a husband?" Mike stumbled, the shock in his speech obvious.

"Not legally," Nick admitted. "In the law of the land our relationship never existed, but between us it did. Helen Becton rang me and probed whether I had any interest in reaching out and meeting you. My immediate instinct was to decline the offer. A few days later, I mulled it over and called her back. It's what John would have wanted, it's on his behalf I'm here."

The shock hung in the air around Mike. Gay? Mike's son was always different. He thought John enjoyed reading and playing games because he was one of the nerdy kids. Mike wanted John to be like him and David, play sports and do manly stuff. But gay? Such a statement jarred with any image he possessed of his youngest son.

"Do you have any proof?" Mike asked, still unsure of the situation that greeted him.

Nick pulled a smartphone out of his pocket and handed the lock screen to Mike. The screen displayed a collage of two photos side by side. The man before him and John in matching blue suits beaming into the camera on the left-hand photo, and kissing a moment later on the right-hand photo. Although Mike heard of fake images and cropping jobs, the wedding day photos appeared real as far as he could tell.

"Where are you from, lad?"

"We lived in Rothbury."

"Rothbury?" Mike gasped. "That's half an hour away."

Nick responded with an awkward smile. Aware of his surroundings, he glanced between Mike and the front door. "Should we go inside?"

Mike nodded, apologised and beckoned a hand for Nick to walk through the front gate. Panic set in as soon as he opened the front door. The home in which he lived returned to chaos as soon as he returned from London. Food wrappers, clothes and dirt lined the hallway floor and Mike swallowed his shame as he led Nick into his kitchen.

"Tea or coffee?" Mike quizzed as Nick moved clothes off a chair.

"Tea would be great," Nick responded. Facial expressions gave nothing away, but Mike knew that everything the man eyeballed only backed up any preconceptions further.

As the kettle boiled, Mike attempted small talk. "So Helen asked you to come?"

"Apparently you have been trying to learn more about your son. Digging in places those in power would rather you didn't. The hope on the call would be that a conversation would put demons to rest."

"How come I haven't heard about you before? You weren't at the funeral or the eulogy?"

"I'm a secret people would rather keep out of sight, which suited us fine."

Mike nodded and focused back on the tea and coffee duties. Assembling a combination of mugs, tea bags and a coffee pot, he set to work. A minute later, a cup of tea in one hand and a mug of coffee emerged. Putting them before Nick, Mike joined him on a seat at the kitchen table.

"So tell me about yourself," Mike fumbled for the words. After all the search for answers, he never expected them to sit opposite with a cup of tea.

"I play rugby on weekends, enjoy long walks in the hills or down the coast when I can. During the week I work in a bookshop in Alnwick – Barter Books, which is where John and I met."

"You don't sound like you're from around here?"

"No," Nick admitted with a smile, like he heard it a thousand times a day. "I grew up near Bristol and went to Northumbria University to study business. I joined an outdoor society during my studies there and loved going for weekend outings to the Northumbrian countryside. Eventually I decided putting down roots up here seemed a good fit. The bookshop work allowed me a stable job when I could go walking on weekends."

Mike nodded as he swigged his coffee. Decades in, Northumberland and the concept of walks on the beach or hikes in the hills never appealed. Then something obvious entered his mind. "How have you been coping since John's death?"

For the first time, Nick looked uncomfortable in his seat at the question. The powerful frame slipped. "We got married six years ago, or at least that's when we had a ceremony and exchanged vows. We could never have a civil partnership or a marriage, nothing that could ever be written. We bought a house in my name, lived the dream and were planning our family of our own," Nick said, the words stinging in his mouth.

"The night before he died, we cooked dinner together. A strange thing. Wine, laughter, excellent food. I could tell something was on his mind, a partner's intuition, but it didn't spoil the evening. We went to bed and in the night I remember him waking up. That always happened. In the six years, I can't remember many times where we went to bed together and woke up that way. John was always coming in late or dashing off before I awoke.

"This time, though, he was talking to me. In my head it's a half-remembered dream. He stroked my hair, whispered to me how much he loved me. His delicate words were that he thought he'd die a lonely man. How grateful he was to have met me. If there was more I don't remember because the next time I woke up he had gone. When I woke up that morning, I learnt they had found his body."

Nick's voice cracked and his tears welled up in his eyes. There was a rage beneath the surface. His shoulders tightened and his fists gripped up into balls with his jumper sleeves. His voice had changed as he spat the words, forcing them out into the open.

"I knew nobody would come, nobody knew I existed. All I got was one phone call off the lady in charge, asking me what I knew. I told her I knew nothing and just yelled at her before I put the phone down. What the fuck had they done to my John? Now I sit lost in a big empty house that was supposed to be full of my family. But now there is no family in my future. I'm angry because the man I loved is gone, angry because the reason he's gone is why I loved him so much. He *had* to be out there, had to be out there saving people. No nights off, no sleeping beside me for a whole night."

Mike soaked up the statement in a room that had suddenly become a vacuum. "I drink," were the only words forthcoming. "When John was a child, when John left, now John's gone. All the way through it, around it, all I do is drink. Not for fun, pleasure or company. I gulp down the self-destructing poison because I am blind to any other existence."

Nick's eyes concentrated on Mike. Shabby clothes, a mess of a house. A pair of eyes flicked to needle-marks on Mike's arms. Like father, like son. Both men silently acknowledged a new addiction had moved in. "John had the same problem."

"John had been clean seven years, they tell me he had fallen off the wagon at the time of his death," Nick continued, a darkness falling over his expression and tone. "When we first met, I knew exactly who John was. How could you not? This superhero standing before my shop's bookshelves, reading the blurbs. Our eyes met and I got a certain vibe from him. That he was interested in me that way, you know? I grew a pair of balls I didn't think I had and asked him for a coffee. In my shock, he accepted."

Nick paused and took a sip of his coffee. "Who I met bettered any pre-conceived ideas I held. Bright, articulate and optimistic, yet shy and anxious all melded in. The self-destruction etched over every inch of his body. I'd met people like him before, almost always an addiction to settle them. Out for coffee, a cosy night in watching a film or a walk in the countryside, John never settled. This rattle of anxiety constantly bounced in his mind. The only thing he had in his locker to soothe it were painkillers and drugs of that nature. Something to blur the rough edges of what he saw. I think no one ever thinks of that? The post-traumatic stress he absorbed daily. The bodies, death and destruction from morning to night.

"We dated, we struggled, but I like to think I helped give him something to come home to. My John loved life. He had a home and a person who loved him and had been sober since the day he proposed. They say one bad day can change the world. It breaks my heart that I'll never know what broke him."

Nick's conversation trailed off as he sipped the tea. No grimace in his expression gave Mike hope that his tea-making skills were okay. Yet the words of Nick haunted him the longer they lingered. Offering someone a home to come back to, shared with a loved one. Maggie, David and John lived and died with no concept of what that could be like.

"He hated me."

"He did," Nick admitted. "You tormented him every day of his childhood and it haunted him, probably as much as it haunts you now. He remembered every time you said slurs in his presence. Every time you tried to make him act less gay. The days you would make fun of him and call him a poof for hating sport and getting scared at night. John hated you for all that, but human beings are capable of more than one emotion. Deep down he loved you because, as much as the hate rooted itself to his core, he knew who you were."

"I used to throw rocks at gays. I made those kids lives a living hell in school. I've hated gay people for as long as I can really remember, and I honestly don't know why. Part of me still sees you as an inhuman person, to be gay. Something hard-wired to stop me accepting them, you, as real, normal people."

"You're not the only one who has thought that way, or still does," Nick acknowledged. "I was lucky – I came out at sixteen and have two loving parents who have accepted me for who I am. Yet for every one of me, I have witnessed dozens in the community with stories like you and John. Parents who see homosexuality as a betrayal of religion, betraying the normal or their healthy upbringings. I've met teenagers from traditional homes where the parents have zero conception of being born gay, their opinion being that you make a choice to engage in it. They threw one friend of mine out."

All that Mike had recalled and relived over the past month made him no better than the other stories. If John came out as gay in his teenage years, the reaction would have been much the same. Time dissolved the energy Mike wished to pump into such hatred.

"Do you hate me?" Mike asked after some hesitation.

"I don't know you," Nick confirmed as he met Mike's eye. "For a decade I heard enough to paint my own picture, and a lot of what I've seen today confirms it. The longer time goes by, the more I stop seeing the black and white of people. We're fucked-up little creatures, too clever to be animals but not clever enough to make sense of it all. I came because Helen asked me to, and I was curious. I think I've seen enough to close one door."

The sense that time was slipping away, and the conversation drawing to a close, taunted Mike. A single moment that would not to be repeated. Once Nick walked out the door, there would not be a second conversation. Had he asked all he could?

"There's a letter, one he left behind to give you should anything happen," Nick mentioned as he got to his feet. "All he told me was to make sure it got to you in person, never through any official channels, and to wait long enough for the heat to die down."

"He knew he could die?"

A thousand mysteries lay behind the husband's eyes. The

answer seemed obvious as soon as he mentioned it. Mike recalled staring down at his son's body in the morgue, scars and a tattoo all over his chest. John *could* switch his abilities off, he could die. That prompted the last question. "What did the tattoo signify?"

"Our wedding day," Nick smiled as a light returned to his eyes for a moment. "John could never wear a ring, part of the secret. We had a ceremony between us. The government would have never allowed a certificate or anything official, even when it became legal for gay men. We made our own vows that meant the same. The tattoo on his chest kept the moment close to his heart."

Once he'd waved the car goodbye, Mike entered his home and left the envelope on the table. He didn't want to open it. The unexpected letter. On instinct, his hand rarely rested on his chest as he took a seat on the sofa, letter in another room. The fear was that the letter would confirm everything he already knew. That he had failed as a father and his son had died hating him.

Yet with every moment that passed, with every task Mike began and abandoned in an effort at distraction, the weight of the envelope in the other room weighed heavier. He would need somebody to read it for him.

Half an hour later and a cup of coffee before him once again, Mike sat in Linda's kitchen. One last letter, he had warned as she opened the front door. That was enough of an explanation for Linda to welcome Mike into her home a second time.

A nervous air before the pair, Linda asked if Mike was sure he wanted her to be the one to read it. Mike confirmed he did. She had done more to earn an ending to the story, whatever the contents may contain. He reiterated his gut feeling. Why would an immortal man write a goodbye letter if he never planned to leave? With delicate words and care, Linda read aloud.

To Dad,

I think in every young boy's life there comes a moment when he compares his father to another, and questions what it is to be a man. I know I have repeatedly done so across my life, from the playground, to teenage years and into adulthood. For those crucial first couple of decades in our lives, our fathers are one of the few men we have to model ourselves against. Little boys lost in the confusion and the noise have a person so much wiser and older to look up to. Fatherhood is priceless in its impact. Good fathers, bad fathers, those absent and the majority somewhere in-between, the influence of such a figure can never be reversed. Today I'm writing you this letter because for so many years I hated you, but the time has come to forgive.

On the school yard I was alone a lot. Other kids never really made sense, and I never had the natural urge to join in their games. Many boys played football on the concrete, inspired by the matches they'd watch with fathers and role models they'd see on the television screens. I never cared for football much and you never took me to games. I guess this was one of the first times I compared you, our relationship, and how we did things differently to other kids. I'd see fathers greeting their boys on the playground while you waited at home, and I made my way back with David. But I loved you in other ways, so it never really mattered to a little boy.

Maturity widened my ability to process what was going on around me. As I entered my teenage years, I became able to see you in a much more critical sense. Age revealed the father I never questioned to have a nasty streak, the fact he had a favourite son and an alcohol problem became clear and all this happened in a period of life where I was trying to make sense of it all. Who was I? What would I become? Who did I want to be? I lost my mother and without her I had you alone to help shape and mould me. For most of my life I believed you failed me on this front – but now I recognise your role as much more complicated.

David's death was the signal of the end of our relationship. The golden child, he would have been a star, wouldn't he? Good grades, handsome with a real aptitude for sport, even being in his shadow was still inspiring. The brighter his flame, the taller mine felt too. And then one day I found him like that. I never could quite believe that his mind had been so dark and brutal. It stole the last bit of light from you. A wife and a son with only me left. I know that you wished it was me; you told me enough times during the drunk rampages and abuse. Those years taught me how to endure, the kids at school who bullied or the negative voice in my head could never compete, and I learnt how to survive.

After all these years, I told nobody how I first discovered my ability. I guess people just accepted it and presumed I did too. On a Thursday afternoon I walked out of school early, to nobody really noticing. You weren't home, the pub, I suspect. No note, I ran myself a hot bath and let myself slip in. I researched the idea well enough, a bottle full of pills swallowed to thin the blood, the boiling water to open the capillaries. I snapped a razor and dragged the blades up the arm, not across, to maximise the impact. By the time I was passing out, I wasn't really focusing on anything at all. The hate, pain and anger I had towards yourself and the world. I didn't feel I fit in and wanted to go out like David, the only real friend I had. There was something romantic in that sense.

The horror was when I woke up. Alone in a freezing cold bath with scarlet-coloured water, it horrified me and I thought myself in some kind of hell. That hell was a return to my reality. Not a scratch or a bruise on me, I had completely healed. I frantically cleaned and wiped the scene. In the darkness of the next few days, my head pounded with confusion. I couldn't feel pain, I would heal in a matter of moments and I had no support network in which to discover myself. Suicide was my ultimate way out, and the door had turned out to be closed with an unbreakable lock.

After the shock came a period of acceptance, and you noticed the change. No matter what abuse you threw I could take it – even when verbal turned to physical I proved uncrushable. The kids at school felt the reaction too. Born again, I fought back. Six of them? It didn't matter. I may not have been strong enough to win, but I had enough spirit and ability to never lose and never stay down.

Our last argument, I suspect you don't even remember. One in the morning, you came staggering in drunk, threw up in the downstairs toilet and your piss hit everywhere but the bowl. As I hauled you to the sofa, you were twisting the knife as you loved to do, evil in your verbal assault. The ending line was one I shrugged off but would later find crushing. "I wish it was you who died". The next morning I left and never came home.

In the years to follow, I had a lot of reflecting to do between the waves of anger. Twisted up, a rage-filled young man, I tried to pretend the life before never existed and started afresh. Denial proved impossible though, and as I struggled through my life, making my own mistakes where I only had myself to blame, I learned to view the world with clearer eyes.

When I pictured you, I recognised a figure haunted by demons I would never fully understand. Alcohol was how you coped with the world, mollified the day-to-day existence and any spikes in your emotion. Painkillers, heroin proved to be my demon to battle and one I fight to this day. Your words would prove haunting as they forever lingered in my mind. I cannot comprehend the situation of a man that could say such a thing to his son, and the bitter irony of wishing death upon an immortal soul.

Yet over the years I have found peace with you. I only hope you became less haunted by the demons that plagued you as a person and a father. I am glad to say eventually I found my purpose and happiness in my way, a life with a meaning to cling to.

Why I write the letter today has a selfish element. Recently I've taken the time to reflect, step back from it all, and I want to tackle my last demon. I'm writing this letter to tell you I forgive you for all the sins you may have perpetrated in the past. The rage, the coping mechanism and the voices in your head were more complicated than I will ever be able to comprehend. I write this letter which will find you when you need it most, and I hope that it is enough to show you I recognise you not just as a father, but as a human being and a person.

There is a quote I want to leave you with. You always hated books, reading and art, but I guess you will have to let me have this one. Viktor Frankl was a Holocaust survivor and writer, and said that "When we can no longer change a situation, it challenges us to change ourselves". In times of hardship I have found these words a great help, and now I'm giving them to you. I forgive you; I love you and I hope you find peace.

Your son,

John

The silence within the walls of the house in Bellington were deafening. Repeatedly Linda reread the words upon Mike's request, his son's voice thick in his brain. With every passing line, the tightness in his chest and mass on his shoulders loosened. Before he died, John had forgiven him.

"Are you okay?" Linda asked with real concern as she put down the letter.

In silence, they sat for what felt like hours. Eventually with a weak smile Linda suggested that maybe Mike head home. He did, and for a long time Mike found himself alone in his front room. There were two roads that lay before Mike: the path of self-destruction he was on and the tougher one that had now opened up to him.

Drenched in sweat, like every pore in his body had opened up, nauseousness and dizziness held Mike. In his front room his body was rejecting itself, going haywire. Mike's stomach twisted in knots, muscles aching, as his body begged to crawl out itself. Mentally and physically, he had come undone.

Wave after wave of emotion swept over Mike. Chaotic thoughts, buried so deep, bubbled forwards. David, John, Maggie. All their faces cold and gone on the autopsy table. The years of vomit down toilet bowls, falls and sorrow.

Bellington, the damn town that had gripped him from birth and never let him out. But it wasn't the town, a place of good people. It was Mike; it had always been Mike. As his body pleaded to go to Rust's and keep all the unravelling at bay, another part of himself forced to remain on the sofa. Had the letter, the forgiveness, changed anything? Did Mike really have anything to live for down the road? Was there still time? Something left in the broken tank?

"I forgive you; I love you and I hope you find peace," Mike repeated as he wept.

Chapter Twenty

For over a month Juliet heard nothing. No messages, no communication or a hint of progress. The cases kept coming with no mention of the hotel room conversation or John Fitzgerald. The idea the entire conversation had been a ploy by Helen to force Juliet off the case crossed her mind several times. Yet the answers provided so much detail, and came so openly, that Juliet couldn't believe in an idea of deceit. Daily she remained busy, patient for her opportunity to get the truth.

A security guard for protection now trailed Juliet wherever she went. Attacks on those who possessed abilities hit the news regularly in other countries. The Marco Rossi incident terrified the public. Now Juliet's own government and employer spoke of registration acts. The public debated cures. Once she tried to raise the issue with her new partner, but he dismissed it, snapping the conversation to a halt. Juliet didn't raise the topic again.

The call came on a standard Tuesday. Prepped in a police station, Juliet expected the morning to concern a series of stabbings in the area. Abruptly, the call shelved those plans. Juliet expected to meet Helen, but they instructed one figure, a driver rather than an agent, to transport her to the care facility.

The conversation thin, part of the instructions, Juliet spent most of the journey anxious as she imagined the scenarios play out. There could be no plan for a girl who dreamt the future.

On the journey Juliet tried to keep track of passing signs, but they displayed unknown towns and villages. Alice's care facility far away from any prying eyes. Dry concrete views drifted into flourishing countryside and after two hours, the roads narrowed.

Only at one side of a two-way mirror did Juliet get her first glimpse at the child she was to interview. In a hospital gown, hair cut short and tied back, Alice appeared every bit an ordinary girl. Hands on the table with the palms laying flat, she stared only forward, an empty vessel as far as Juliet could see. Yet despite the unnerving display, Juliet could see the youth in her features, the delicate thinness of her wrists and body. Outside of context and situation, the girl would not be out of place in a classroom or playground.

"There's talk in the media of bringing in a registration act," Helen declared from beside Juliet as she too looked at the child. "I have no idea how long we can keep the existence of Alice a secret if it's brought in. The choice would be open rebellion against the government or adding fuel to the fire."

"You really think they'd hurt a child?"

"World events are changing fast, Juliet," Helen acknowledged. "Past any act, we will continue to tighten borders and the Prime Minister will lose his leadership election. Hell, I know they'll replace me before too long. I hope I have time to get answers before I go."

"She's just a girl," Juliet repeated her thought aloud. "A little girl who can dream the future would mess anybody up inside."

"Like being able to read minds?"

Juliet glanced at Helen. An entire career in her employment and this encounter, off the record and as unofficial as possible, would be only a handful they'd ever shared. Abilities shaped their owners more than Helen could ever know. Yet abilities altered more than just the individuals. Every person Juliet encountered had a preconceived notion of what she would be like, even her boss. The abilities defined those like Juliet and Alice.

Juliet headed for the room's entrance and took one last breath. Nerves now seized her. All the answers to everything that remained surrounding John Fitzgerald sat in the little girl's mind. If Juliet failed, so did any hope of learning the truth.

The instant Alice's eyes locked onto Juliet, the power dynamic of the conversation became clear. The facility, the guards, and the agents covering the doors meant nothing. The true power lay in the dark-haired girl's head, waiting in the interview room. As Juliet entered the room, she felt ill as she felt herself become submissive to a little child, the conversation occurring on her terms and on her turf.

Alice's eyes stood out the most as they rested, unflinching. The entire face carried the weight of an adult's, utter confidence and an unwavering sureness in her gaze. The colour of her eyes was grey like smoke, and a complex machine ticked behind the blank expression. Every rare blink appeared timed and planned. The appearance gave nothing away, but contempt lingered from the firm lips to the rigid eyebrows. As her stomach swam and her instincts screamed danger, Juliet knew in her heart that Alice held the control.

The contrast between an eleven-year-old girl and the restraints that bound her remained startling. Real or imagined, the temperature of the room dropped in Alice's company, as if Alice was a black hole sapping happiness and life from the atmosphere. Juliet had met many bad people in her time, from rapists to murderers. Alice was the first person who dripped hatred and where the word 'evil' felt not in the slightest hyperbolic.

"I drew you a picture," Alice stated as Juliet took a seat. Flicking a bound hand, she slid a drawing across the table. Childlike, poorly crafted, the pencilled image showed Juliet with her arms drooping. Blood poured from a heavy wound as she hung from what looked to be a meat hook. "I give it a year before they come for you."

Juliet slid the drawing back across the table. She would only speak when she had a read of the situation. Juliet hadn't yet dared turn on the tap and get inside Alice's brain fully, for fear of showing how unnerved she was. Something felt wrong and unlike anything she had experienced in someone's head before.

"I dreamt you would come," the girl's voice cracked through the silent room. There was a childlike edge to it, but time had worn the hint away. Efficient, brutal and cold, each word had a slight cut to it. "You've come to ask why I murdered John Fitzgerald and you'll leave once you have your answers."

"You know why he died?" Juliet asked.

"I have never met a mind-reader before. I find it interesting that John never learnt how your ability ticked. I want to explore you. A question for a question."

There was real menace in Alice's expression now. Her clouded eyes wanted to rip inside her head and swim in any trauma they found. The individual opposite getting even the slightest peek into her mind frightened Juliet. Yet this was the closest opportunity for the truth a person would ever get.

"I'll play your game," Juliet agreed and then continued. "Go first."

"Tell me about your relationship with your daddy."

"He was kind, a good father," Juliet answered.

Alice tutted and tapped her head. "I don't believe that. A mind-reader being able to hear every thought of her parents, every time they're disappointed or angry. I know that would scar. My daddy stopped visiting years ago. After they put me in here, I dreamt he would have an affair. The enjoyment was keeping quiet on that one. With every parental visit, I looked for the signs until I could confirm to myself that he'd done it. The look on both their faces when I revealed he'd had his cock in the neighbour's cunt. You should have seen it. My favourite, I laughed for months. He rarely came back and eventually my mother stopped too…"

"He loved her more than me," Juliet interrupted. "I remember on my sixteenth birthday, the early days of my power emerging, that he loved his wife more than his daughter. He came to hug me and the thought just popped into his mind. Nothing to trigger it. He hugged me and the thought in his mind was that he loved me, was proud of me. Yet behind that mask he loved his wife and wished for the embrace of her more. It didn't matter what I did, how much I loved him – I would never be good enough to outshine her love."

Alice smirked. "John had daddy issues too; I think we all do. Doesn't matter how good or caring they are over a lifetime, there will be one misplaced comment, a stinging argument somewhere. We tell ourselves they're human, parents make mistakes, but in reality it still burns. Parents are the holy grail of perfection, and their opinions will always matter."

Outside, dozens of agents listened to every word of the conversation, desperate for any intelligence Alice could give. The reality of the conversation in the room jarred with how it looked from the outside. To them, the encounter involved an adult speaking to a child. Inside the room, Juliet knew no childlike innocence remained. But she knew better than to waste a question.

"Why did John let himself die?"

"A question with too many layers," Alice retorted. "This is a game, not a race to the finish. Have fun! I'll help you out. Let's see if you, as a detective of sorts, can figure it all out yourself. Why would John come in the first place? Well Juliet, after saving the world for over a decade, John had saved millions of lives. Yet John also missed saving the lives of millions by being in the wrong place at the wrong time. The United Nations did their best in putting him where he needed to be, but there were so many missed opportunities. Every time there was a mudslide in Afghanistan, John remained geographically absent for a fire in Beijing. Little John couldn't save them all and it tore his self-esteem apart. Appetite gone, insomnia because of his experiences, he sought a little girl in a mental institute because he wanted to dream about the future too. Two months later and he's being stabbed to death with his permission."

"What did he dream?" Juliet asked on instinct.

"My turn," Alice corrected. "Tell me about your love life."

A lump formed in Juliet's throat. Had any of the conversation been news to the little girl, or had Juliet just been an actor reading from a screenplay? Outside, Juliet could read the thoughts of the hovering agents. They judged and waited for the reply. Rather than being alone in the room, Juliet suffered on a stage in front of an audience. The cost of the truth would be her dignity. The tapes to be replayed a thousand times by anonymous accusers. "I don't have one, I haven't dated ever, really."

"Juicy," Alice beamed, and within a flash her eyes were pressing for more. "Go on."

"From the age of sixteen there's been no off tap for other people. Any friend I ever had, I'm exposed to them at their worst. If they want to maintain a relationship with me at all. People become freaked out at the prospect of having their innermost thoughts exposed. So I'm alone mostly, I run and work-out and stick to solo sport that doesn't need other people. Dating-wise? How can I ever be intimate with someone, trust someone, when I know every white lie they ever tell?

"Even a month back, a man began chatting to me in a queue for coffee. Flirting, but not heavily, I could hear his attraction in his thoughts. He seemed genuine, nice and for a little while I genuinely considered taking him up on his advance. But as I was paying, still in front of him in the queue, he considered whether his ex would be jealous if rocked up to a friend's wedding with me on his arm. Right there, as always, I hear the truth. On some level, any relationship I'd have with this man would be predicated on revenge. So I stay alone, I like it that way, it keeps things simple."

Juliet's stomach churned after her latest confession. It exposed a queasy uncertainty as Alice ripped layers off her. But she had to be strong if she dallied or delayed – there was the very real possibility that the game could end with no answers beyond the basics.

"The only person on the planet who can read minds," Alice echoed. "Lonelier than anyone."

"What did John dream in those final two months?" Juliet

replied firmly.

"The future," Alice laughed. "And it's not very nice for us."

"Us?"

"What links the two stories you just told me? The story about your father, the lack of relationships?"

Juliet genuinely had no answer.

"A little girl dreams the future, she ends up in a mental asylum. An Italian man can shoot fire out of his hands, we encourage the violence in him. The world's lone mind-reader mistrusted and kept isolated. John, the best of us, unable to live his life out in the open," Alice acknowledged out loud. "They fear us, the normal people out there. Maybe they should."

"But how does that link to the dreams?"

"John hoped to witness upcoming incidents and disasters, thus being in the right place to stop them. Dreaming about the future doesn't work like that. The visions work like normal dreams, unplanned and erratic. The future John saw involved humanity making those with super-abilities extinct. They turn on us, on him, and it gets nasty. Talk of forced cures and registrations. Very Hitler, very Holocaust. Eventually it hits a breaking point and we fight back, John fights back and the war to follow kills a billion. It's not just us versus them. That would be too black and white. Populations take sides and civil wars erupt. It's like being a witch back in the old days – drownings, burnings and crucifixions. Before too long, we forget what it is we're really fighting for. It's survival. John spent two months dreaming about that future in his head before it all got too much."

At this stage Juliet, Juliet's mind was a mess, her self-esteem in tatters. Behind the glass and the recordings, individuals she didn't even know would study her, this interview and this encounter for years. Juliet's greatest shame, insecurities and her innermost life laid bare for examination.

"From what I've seen, the case has obsessed you, consumed your life and every waking moment. Why are you miserable? Why have you chased this so hard?"

"To learn if the burden of this ability is all worth it," Juliet admitted with as much honesty she could muster. "I have dedicated ten years of my life to investigating crimes. Murder, violence or terrorism offences. Every day, I sit on one side of a glass interview room attempting to get into the heads of those under suspicion. A decade is a long time to spend inside the thoughts of terrible men. Every day a new man enters, takes a seat, and I hear all about the evil and rage in his acts. And you know what? The seat never stays empty for long. I often loathe my ability, the path it has forced me down. The only thing I can cling to is that, somehow, it serves a purpose I have stopped seeing."

"Well, you'll like my next answers," Alice laughed. "Go on. Ask why John let himself die? It's about time."

"He thought his death could stop the apocalypse, the one you both dreamt. Somehow bring humanity together?"

"Close," Alice acknowledged. "But a biblical optimism. No, John did not die selfless or a martyr for humanity's future. That's still a little too optimistic. John understood the inevitable truth. No matter how big, how strong or how powerful he became, nothing can stop human nature. A plaster to a far bigger wound. Humanity cannot tackle the root cause of the pain. Resources run thin, individualism takes over and humanity tears itself apart. We cannot stop the dark future to come. The truth took a while, but when John got the reality into his thick, confident head he checked himself out – the biggest player in the game removed his participation. He knew we need to lose."

The answer stunned a drained Juliet to silence.

"If you think this story has a happy ending, you haven't been paying attention to the news," Alice said as her commanding laughter returned.

"Why murder and not suicide?" Juliet threw her last question into the mix as the realisation dawned on her. "He used Casper like a prop. Why couldn't the coward just do it himself?"

"A suicide raises questions that demand an explanation. A murder by a drug addict? Nobody bothers to seek the explanation, and they never trust the one they get. This truth you've heard, the genocide to come, they'll allow it to happen. We're both dead and there's no way to stop it. They wipe us out. John just made sure that the death toll remains a few hundred rather than a billion. Humanity steps out of the dark chapter unscathed and can finish the book. He was their true saviour."

As Juliet glared at Alice, she took a moment to dip into her head. Every word had been the truth. The face she stared into, with the clouded eyes, pale skin and devilish grin laughed once more. A deep, conceited and manic laughter Juliet could no longer tolerate. Throwing her chair back, Juliet stormed out of the room, leaving the melody of hysteria behind her.

Tears streamed down Juliet's face and as others came to approach her, she shoved them away. Her frustration boiled into anger. Through the crowd she eyeballed Helen, even the figure of absolute control forced into uncertainty. Juliet's wrath turned in her direction.

"How many of us are there?" Juliet screamed at Helen, sympathetic rather than cold for the first time since they'd met.

"Three hundred and sixty-two individuals with known super-ability traits across the globe," Helen stammered. Her eyes flicked between needing to meet Juliet's and avoiding them.

Three hundred and sixty-two murders to stop a war that would kill billions. They were all like lambs destined for slaughter.

"Did you know?" Juliet barked at Helen, but the thoughts bubbling in her mind revealed the truth. The revelation from inside the room was news to the ears of anybody listening. John instigated his murder to save humanity from itself.

Beyond the scenes in the room, Juliet questioned the brutal logic. The philosophy reminded her of an injured human's limb being amputated to save the rest of the body. Yet had the doctor considered the endgame? The poison in the body deep enough to rot a limb – did the removal secure survival? Maybe humanity limped on longer, but how long for? Did the dreams reveal the eventual cost?

Juliet stormed away from the crowd of agents and intelligence personnel that gathered, their thoughts and voices distant as their attention fixated on the events in the room. The truth repeated in Juliet's mind. The death of John Fitzgerald had been closer to a suicide than a murder investigation. In an act of cowardice, John opted to die rather than fight the future emerging across the globe. Could Juliet do the same? At some unknown point, the public would come for her. An angry mob through the streets, to come and kill her and impale her on hooks. All to eradicate an ability in her body she never chose, never asked for.

A fire exit stood before Juliet, a single door between the

facility and the outside world. Beyond the cold metal, a world changing its nature and priorities awaited. Juliet pushed other voices and thoughts to the side. Only her own monologue mattered. Thoughts and feelings mattered now, as the voices of all those nearby dimmed. Could she do it, wait to die?

Or would she fight back?

Printed in Great Britain
by Amazon